Sexual Secrets and Erotic Encounters

real stories told by real couples

Edited by Nora Steel

"It's perfectly natural, extremely pleasurable, and enhances your relationship. So live, love, learn about it. Sex. Do your body good."

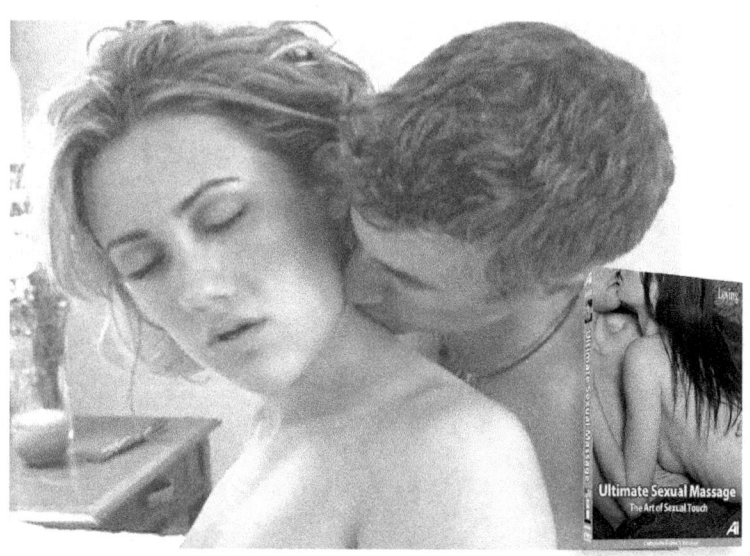

FREE DVD offer on page 152

Published by
Alexander Institute, Inc.
15124 Ventura Blvd.
Suite 206
Sherman Oaks, CA 91403
www.lovingsex.com
818-508-1296

10 9 8 7 6 5 4 3 2 1

Library of Congress Cataloging-in-Publication Data available.

Table of Contents

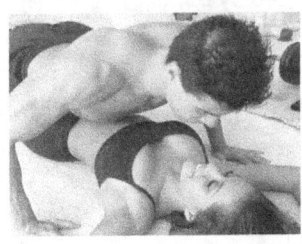

82 Part 2 - WHAT WOMEN WANT

4

INTRODUCTION

What does your partner want when it comes to sexuality? How do they like to be touched? Do they like it when you stroke them faster or slower? Stimulate their G-Spot or their clit? Lick their nipples softly or give them a good tweak? Do they like rough play or gentle lovemaking? Deep thrusts or shallow petting? Frequent sex or a languid build-up of tension in between? What are their fantasies? Do they like role play... dirty talk... sex toys... sharing with a third party?

No matter how well you know someone, you may not know the answers to these questions unless you ask.

Good sexual communication is difficult. It requires honesty, patience, and listening - to both words and body language. Note what makes your partner pull away or pull you closer. Recognize the difference between a moan of pleasure and a sigh of resignation. Letting your lover know what does and doesn't work for you is an ongoing process, and it's one that will ultimately make your relationship closer than ever.

The sexually adventurous couples in the following erotic stories are open-minded and non-judgmental about trying new things and finding new ways to please their partners. They are excited about expanding their sex lives as a way of improving their relationships overall. We hope they will encourage you to listen to your partner, learn what to ask and how to ask it, and lead an improved love life of incredible sex!

Sexual Secrets & Erotic Encounters

Real couples. Real sex. Real life.

Part 1

What Men Want

Here's what some of the men we spoke to said:

"I look for honesty and open communication. I want to be able to say what I want to say and expect that back from my partner."

"At this point in my life, I'm looking for a commitment. Basically, I'm looking for a relationship that's going to lead to a serious commitment that's going to lead to marriage."

"Excitement, steadfastness, flexibility, love."

"I like being romantic, because when I'm romantic, Diane really responds."

"A quick relationship sexually is like a shallow well. I'd rather dig deep and get to know a woman."

"She has to be smart, she has to know what she's about, and she has to know what she wants. I go for very intelligent. Very intelligent women are usually my choice because they seem to know a little bit more about what's going on."

6

"I find the most appealing thing to me in a relationship is the care that's there between two partners. The sensitivity about feelings and companionship... being together."

"I'd say initiation on their part I find very attractive."

"I like a self-assertive woman, you know... aggressiveness. That gives me reassurance that she wants me."

"I like it when she takes me out on a date, you know. When a woman finally takes you out on a date...be in charge, I like that."

"When a woman wants you too much and shows it right away, sometimes it takes that feeling of a challenge away. So if she's too sexually assertive too soon, sometimes it makes you back off a little."

"A little bit of inventiveness."

"Sex in the shower can be really hot. You take a shower in the morning with your partner and just start fucking."

"I love being seduced, because Anna is really good at it."

"My wife is the best seductress in the world. She likes to play these little games. And I know a few, too!"

~~~

In the first story, you'll see how much Tina's husband loves it when she gets creative…

Brad & Tina
Stairway to Heaven

My wife, Tina, really knows how to blow my mind. I don't know how she comes up with some of her ideas but she's damn good. She keeps me wondering what's next. It's exciting knowing that every time we fall into a comfortable pattern and I least expect it, she'll spring some kind of sexy surprise on me.

Like the night in question. I came home expecting my routine greeting from Tina, who's usually in the kitchen, ready to eat and waiting for me by the time I get there.

But the house was quiet, and Tina didn't answer when I called for her. I thought she must be upstairs, and when I went to look I saw a paper lying on the bottom step. I picked it up, and Whoa! It was a photo of two lovely breasts.

When I was able to tear my eyes away from that lovely sight I realized the entire staircase was strewn with surprises. Right above the photo of those two delicious breasts was a picture of Tina wearing my favorite pair of her bikini underwear. She

8

had it pulled aside to reveal her lovely pussy. My mouth watered. This was definitely not the greeting I was expecting after a tough day at work... but it was a welcome one!

On the third step there was no photo... but her sexy black lace thong was lying there. I climbed further and there was a picture of Tina wearing a revealing white teddy, an outfit that's another one of my favorites. Is it too corny to say this was turning into a Stairway to Heaven? Yeah, it is, but it was definitely getting me horny.

As I continued climbing the stairs, another picture awaited me. Oh my, my. In the photo Tina was posed sitting with one hand squeezing her breast and the other hand stroking her pussy. That photo made my dick come alive. And there were more goodies waiting. Tina's bra was on the next step. On the one after that was a photo of her pleasuring herself with her favorite dildo. In the final photo Tina was bent over showing off her butt... and my wife has a very nice butt! My dick was hard as a rock now as I stared at the pictures and stroked her silky lingerie.

I wore a big smile on my face as I entered our bedroom teasingly calling Tina a very bad girl. But Tina wasn't there. I thought she might be waiting for me in our Jacuzzi tub but she wasn't in the master bathroom either. "Where the hell is she?" I wondered. I headed to the guest bedroom thinking maybe she wanted a change of venue. She wasn't in bed there either, but I heard water running.

Tina was in the shower, lathering creamy white soap bubbles all over her body. The fragrance was fresh and clean. She smiled when she saw me and I told her how much I loved the photos. She leaned against the shower door and rubbed her tits back and forth on it, making soapy white streaks on the glass. She looked so damn sexy. I pressed against the outside of the door and said it looked like she was having a lot of fun in there. Tina had a very mischievous look on her face. She pushed open the shower door, grabbed my arm and pulled me into the shower, clothes and all!

She was grinding her body against me even as I struggled to get my soaking wet shirt off. She slid her breasts across my chest, the touch of her perky little nipples making my body tingle. I took her in my arms and kissed her, caressing her shoulders and back. My hands drifted down to her tight butt. Tina has really nice thighs, and she loves when I stroke them, so I turned her around and pulled her back against me, rubbing the silky lather down along the front of her thighs.

Tina got the shower gel and squeezed some on my chest, rubbing it all over me. Then she bent over and yanked my pants down, which at this point were a sopping wet mess. She had a naughty grin on her face as she gathered the lather from my chest and rubbed it on my dick, stroking up and down with a gentle twist.

Tina gives a great hand job, and I was growing thicker and harder with each stroke. She slowly applied more and more pressure, and the slippery soap felt like velvet sliding against me. Watching her work on me and feeling her perfect touch, I had to hold onto the wall. My knees were going weak. I moaned with pleasure, my voice echoing through the shower as I encouraged her to keep doing it, just like that. Tina looked happy that I was enjoying her surprise so much. I held on to her butt and squeezed her breasts.

My dick was throbbing and I had to have her. I lifted her leg and pushed deep into her. It felt so good I had to pause and catch my breath. Then I started pumping and our bodies fell into rhythm. She reached up to kiss me and grabbed my butt, pulling me further into her. It felt like the tip of my cock was deeper inside her than ever before. I grabbed both of her legs and she held onto the shower head. She was panting and

I was gasping for air. I knew I couldn't last much longer.

Tina was in her own world now, driven by inner passions. I looked at her tight butt resting in my hands and her curvy thighs pumping away, and it put me over the top. I exploded. It felt amazing. I was seeing stars. It was one of the best climaxes I ever had.

Afterward, we clung to each other in silence for a few minutes, the warm water from the shower head continuing to flow down our bodies. I lowered her legs, ran my hands up and down her body and kissed her gently. "Let me tell you something, Tina," I said, "I love coming home to you."

~~~

We asked some men a very specific question: What makes a woman good in bed?

"The ability to let go, be uninhibited, and just experiment. Willingness to try things, different positions, oral sex, whatever is the mood."

"I think the sexiest woman is a woman with no inhibitions."

"Body language... sex appeal... her reaction to my touch. That's what I find appealing."

"Janet's really responsive. Even when we're in bed and she comes, and she wants me to stop, I just keep going and going. It drives her nuts all over again."

In the next story, you'll hear how Stephen gets turned on even more when Janet lets him know how much pleasure he's giving her...

11

Stephen & Janet
Naked Sunshine

We have a secluded yard and my wife Janet loves to sunbathe nude by our pool. One day last week, in the middle of a very time-consuming project, I felt myself dragging. I needed a short nap. When I went into the bedroom, I glanced out the window and saw Janet lying outside in the yard on the lounger, not wearing a stitch of clothing. Even in the privacy of our own yard, it amazed me how uninhibited she is. I think she's awesome.

She looked absolutely delicious stretched out so peacefully with nature all around her. Tired as I was, my crotch started to wake up. I stared at my sleeping wife as I slowly undressed. The sun was dipping and a gentle breeze tousled her hair, waking her from the luxury of her afternoon nap. She sat up and rubbed the sleepiness from her eyes.

Refreshed from her forty winks, she stood up and stretched. She has a long lean body and she looked beautiful. She gathered up her pool towel, stepped into her sandals and headed toward the house.

I stretched out on the bed and lay there waiting for her. "Hi there," I said, smiling as she entered the bedroom. I know she was surprised to see me lying nude on the bed because it's rare for me to have a moment like that in the middle of the day. But she smiled like it was business as usual and joined me on the bed. I asked her if she enjoyed her "sun bath", and and she said yes, she loved the warmth of the sun on her bare skin. I winked and told her it looked good too.

Reaching over, I gently stroked her stomach. The heat of the summer sun was still on her soft skin, and the warmth emanating from her body was inviting. I caressed her breasts and she sighed, whispering that she loved my touch. I couldn't resist tasting them, so I planted soft kisses on her breasts to wake her nipples up. I pulled one into my mouth, loving every minute of it.

I was feeling horny now, brushing my nose and face against Janet's skin. That really turns me on. I slowly worked my way around her body, brushing along her chest and down to her stomach. I stopped for a few kisses on her cute little belly button. Then I continued down to her hips and her luscious legs, caressing her outer thighs with my face and then moving on to her inner thighs. As I was savoring the sensation, Janet grabbed my head and flicked her tongue at me. That's her sign to get it on, and I dig it that she can put it out there and let me know when she's in the mood for my tongue. I licked her soft inner thighs. Janet sighed and told me it felt good. When she lets me know what she's feeling it makes me even hornier. I had to taste her.

I climbed between her legs, spread them wide and made love to her pussy with my tongue. Rolling my head from side to side and up and down, I licked, sucked and nibbled on her clit. I was all over her, and I could tell Janet was loving it by her moans.

Her body language told me how much pleasure she felt. She would spread her legs even wider or grab my head and push it in further. Then she'd pull it back out, like she couldn't take any more. She kept telling me how good it felt, moaning and sighing the whole time. She shifted positions, first reaching back to the bedpost so she had something to grab onto, then sliding one leg off the bed and raising her butt. Being in bed with Janet is like riding an unbroken horse. I swear sometimes she's part animal... wild and untamed!

Then, in a flash, she changed it up. Her approach became very soft and sensuous. When she's in that tender mood, I take control again. I like to give her what I call "the magic finger." While I nibble and suck on her clit, I pump my finger in and out of her pussy. It drives her crazy. Janet moaned and twisted her body to the rhythm of my strokes. She tweaked her nipples while I sucked her clit. When I hit her hot spot, she clamped her legs tightly around my head and raised her butt up off the bed.

She was panting and telling me to stop. Every man knows that "stop" means stop... but Janet is my woman and we've discussed the difference between a real "STOP!" and her protests in the middle of sex that really mean "this feels so good I can hardly stand it." I know the difference and so does she. It's actually kinda funny, because the first few times she told me to stop in the heat of passion, I did. And she'd ask me what was wrong... why did I stop?

So I paused just long enough to climb up and kiss her sweet lips. "No problem, baby," I said, "but are you sure you want me to stop?" She said it felt so good she didn't think she could take anymore. And then she said, well, maybe just a little more. I smiled, kissed her again, and moved back down her body. I stuck my finger back in her pussy, found her G-spot and massaged it.

Janet reached for my dick and started stroking it. I was hard as a rock. I kept sliding my finger in and out of her pussy, and she flopped back onto the bed, letting the sensations roll through her. She tilted her body up to encourage my magic finger. Each time I slid into her she rocked from side to side, her legs sliding up and down in response to my movement. She fondled her breasts and thrust her pelvis forward, wailing as a burst of sexual energy erupted from her.

I relinquished her pussy and slid up to suck her nipples again. Janet's breathing was heavy. She kissed me deeply. She whispered that she came really hard, and I told her there was more to come... we weren't done yet. Before she could say another word, I spread her legs wide and thrust my cock deep inside her. She screamed with pleasure as I made long, deep, hard strokes. I pulled almost all the way out of her and then drove it home again. Janet thrust back at me, rockin' her body in rhythm with mine.

Our lovemaking had reached such a frenzied peak that she almost slid off the bed. She kept telling me with each stroke how good it felt and how much she liked what I was doing. The more she talked the harder I pumped in and out of her. Her words were urging me on... harder, deeper, faster. I felt like I could go all night, but finally Janet begged me to stop, just for a minute. I eased up the pace, pumping slower and softer, then paused to kiss her. Janet wrapped her legs around mine and continued to sigh and moan.

Then she pulled away, and said it was her turn. She started massaging her clit and stared at me with a very horny look in her eyes. She commanded me to lie back, and I obeyed. She crawled over to me, positioning herself above my still hard dick. She grasped hold and teasingly savored me like a lollipop. Gently holding it with one hand, she licked me from the base to the tip and back down again. Her lips were soft and juicy and the feeling was incredible. She went up one side and down the other, circling around until every inch of my cock was tingling with delight.

Smiling and stroking it, she slowed down and asked if I liked what she was doing. I told her she was driving me crazy, and she teased that maybe I couldn't take anymore. I told her I could take whatever she wanted to give. Baby, I said, I want it all. That's when she slowly, sensuously slid me into her mouth. Watching her take me in, combined with the touch of her flicking tongue, created a surge of feeling that was almost more than I could bear. I tensed, and she could tell that she was bringing me to climax. But Janet wasn't done teasing me. She pulled me out of her mouth, gave me a devilish look and said, "Not yet!"

She straddled me, reached back and slid her hot wet pussy down onto me. It was ecstasy. She moved up and down slowly and evenly, calming me down and prolonging the pleasure, then picked up the pace. Her eyes were closed and her hand thrown up in the air like she was riding a bucking bronco. Her mouth was open, her teeth were clinched, and her thighs were clamped tightly around my throbbing dick. Oh, she was blowing my mind.

But now it was me who decided, "Not yet." I wasn't ready for this to be over. I had an irresistible desire to taste her again before I came. Even though it felt so good being inside of her, I forced myself to pull out. Flipping her onto her back, I spread her legs wide and plunged back in between her tight thighs. I licked her furiously and pumped my magic finger in and out, in and out. She grabbed my head and launched into her "Stop" routine again, begging me to stop... telling me I was driving her crazy.

But I knew she didn't mean it, so I kept going until she was ready to come again. Before she would let herself go, she pushed me away. Rolling over onto her knees, she presented her backside to me. I could barely stand it. I was already rock hard and the sight of those firm round cheeks looking for action nearly drove me wild. Another dip in her juicy pussy would be ecstasy. I pulled her close, held on to her luscious butt and drove deep inside her.

I knew the floodgates were about to open. My body tensed tighter and tighter as I plunged deeper and deeper. My whole being began to spasm. For one delirious moment Janet and I were suspended in time. Her contractions intensified faster and tighter around my swollen dick. I thrust into her one last time and we both came as hard as we ever had. There was no stopping now for either of us. It was glorious.

Physically and emotionally satisfied, we both fell back on the bed, sighing and moaning. Wow. What a great unexpected break from my work project that was!

~~~

"I'd like to try sex outdoors, but I've never really done that."

"I think any form of sex outdoors is pretty fun... and somewhere there's a chance that you might get caught adds to it. Or on any form of transportation... something like that."

"I think that sex in nature is a wonderful feeling. I mean, to be outside under the warm sun having sex by a stream or on the beach... it's extraordinary. It's a wonderful feeling."

"Basically, the top of the local mountains is what I like. An out-in-nature kind of thing, if you will."

Theo tells how he loves a playful woman with an adventurous spirit...

Theo & Kendra

Sexual Detour

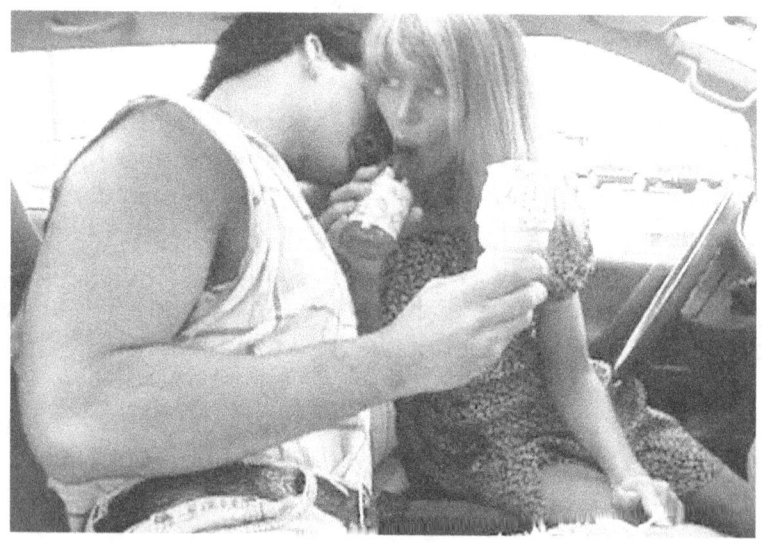

About two weeks ago, my girlfriend Kendra and I took a drive up to Santa Barbara. It was a typical hot sunny Southern California day. The kind of day I like because the women wear less clothing. Kendra was wearing a flimsy little sundress... it hung off her shoulders and skimmed over her breasts and hips. Just watching her walk in it was a turn on.

It was about one o'clock in the afternoon by the time we finally got in the car and headed out. By two o'clock we were both getting a bit hungry and realized we should have eaten something before we left because we wouldn't be there for at least another hour. Kendra was driving and she spotted an ice cream shop in the middle of a small shopping center. That's not the kind of place we would usually stop, but she was in the mood for something sweet.

She pulled into the parking lot and said she'd get us a snack. I was glad she volunteered because I didn't feel like budging out into the heat.

Kendra parked under a big tree at the far end of the lot where there was a bit of shade and hopped out to get her ice cream. I lowered the seat back and closed my eyes for a minute.

I must have dozed off because the next thing I knew Kendra was opening the car door again, holding out and ice cream cone. It looked like the perfect treat for such a hot day. I took it and licked up what was already melting down the sides, then dug in. As she got back in the car she said the sun was sweltering out there.

Her beautiful face was flushed. I touched her cheek and kissed her. "You didn't get overheated, did you?" I asked. She smiled and said she was fine. I noticed she was sitting rather provocatively. She had her body twisted to face me with one leg up, perched on the edge of her seat. I reached over and rubbed that beautiful calf. Kendra works hard at keeping in shape and she has great legs... long, lean, and very shapely. I told her she sure looked cute in that revealing little sundress. She smiled and licked the ice cream suggestively, a naughty look on her face.

One of the straps of the sundress had fallen off her shoulder down onto her upper arm... very sexy. I couldn't resist fondling her breast. Kendra likes to go braless, which I love. She has nice full breasts and as I caressed her the top button on her dress came undone. Her nipple popped out. It looked more delicious than any ice cream could, so I gave it a little squeeze and sucked it into my mouth. I told her she not only looked delicious, she tasted better than ice cream any day. She laughed but I knew she liked the compliment.

I took another lick, savoring her soft skin and perky nipple. It was like having dessert after dessert! I stroked the soft bare skin on her legs, slowly traveling up. I think we were both a little horny because she was rubbing my leg at the same time. She told me she liked the little rips in my jeans, pushing

19

her fingers through the denim holes, tickling my skin under-neath. I grinned like a wolf and told her there was other stuff in my jeans she might like, too. She said she already knew what was in my jeans, and already knew she liked it. She kissed me and started massaging my crotch.

Unzipping me, she reached in and pulled out "Junior", which is her pet name for my cock. The old boy stood right up, sensing something good was about to happen. Kendra gripped it gently and began to stroke. I pressed my back into the seat; the sensation was instant. Her fingers felt like velvet. She kissed the tip and licked it like the ice cream cone. Oh boy, this was an unexpected pleasure!

Remembering where we were, I looked around the parking lot and saw there were other cars parked nearby. Uh-oh...I told her it was nasty doing this in a parking lot. Kendra paused for only a minute and then she swallowed my dick again. She was giving me chills. I didn't want her to stop, so I tried to pretend I was just sitting back in the car listening to the radio. Kendra was sucking like crazy, making love to me with her luscious lips. Her head was bobbing up and down and I was sure it would draw attention if anybody walked by. She paused and told me to act normal while she worked on Junior. Normal? That would be pretty hard to do when I could hardly stop moaning.

Kendra set Junior on fire. It wasn't going to take much more for me to come. But I forced myself to hold back. I gently grabbed her hair and pulled her head up away from me. I told her she was a bad girl and I loved it! But I wanted to make sure nobody was watching. I have an SUV and the windows aren't tinted, so I suggested we move into the back seat where we would be less visible. After we got situated in the back, I asked Kendra to stand up and peek out the sunroof to make sure there weren't any people around. She popped her head up through the open sunroof. She didn't see anybody close by, but sitting behind her while she looked gave me an idea. I told her to stay up there for a minute and keep looking to make sure no one was coming.

I had an ulterior motive, of course. While Kendra played lookout with her head up through the sunroof, I slid my hands under her dress and between her legs. She moaned and said she didn't think that was a good idea. But I knew what I was doing. I told her to just stay calm, everything would be okay. I continued to rub her legs and butt, and slipped my finger into her wet pussy. She moaned quietly. I thrust my finger in and out, and she spread her legs wider. I knew what she wanted, so I stuck my head between her legs and slid my tongue into her silky pussy. I licked and sucked and she moaned again. The more I licked, the wetter she got.... and the hornier I got.

Junior wanted to be in her, and he wanted it right now. I pulled Kendra back into the car and laid her on her back. She looked so luscious. I spread her legs and tasted her again. Let me tell you, her pussy never tasted sweeter. Kendra kept looking out toward the parking lot, worried that each passing car was going to park next to us. But I knew she didn't really care whether or not anybody saw us because she reclined the seat and opened her legs even wider. She wanted it. That really turned me on and I was about to burst. I finally slid Junior into her warm wet pussy. Kendra eagerly received me.

I could tell she was drifting off into her own world. She was lost in the action, her body responding by reflex. I kept popping my head up to check out the parking lot. The feeling of danger was adding to our excitement, but still, I wanted to make sure we didn't get caught! The coast was clear. I got on one knee, sliding in and out between her legs. Kendra was no longer concerned about who might be watching. She was in her zone. The rush from being in her pussy out in public was sending me over the edge.

I didn't care who was looking. It was an out-of-body experience. I was a mass of nerve endings and my pleasure meter was about to blow off the scale. Kendra's whole body heated up. She gripped my ass as tremors shook through her. We held each other, synchronized in a spine-tingling release of sexual tension.

We both moaned, and then remembered we had to try to be quiet. It was tough because I felt like screaming. Kendra pulled my body against her as tight as she could. We both shivered as release washed over us.

We came at the same time, and then collapsed against the car seat. We were both dripping with sweat, but it was a wonderful feeling. I rolled over and fell onto the seat next to her. We looked at each other and started laughing. Had we actually just done that? "Oh baby," I said, "I really like an afternoon drive with you."

~~~

"I like oral sex."

"I guess I'm an exhibitionist; I don't mind somebody watching."

"I really love to have sex in the middle of the day, right at lunch time."

"I like oral sex, but I like giving it more than receiving it."

In the next story, Jack never has a full erection or an orgasm, even when his lovemaking session has the added arousal element of a voyeur. Denise doesn't point it out or ask anxious questions about whether she's turning him on or stimulating him correctly. She simply goes on with her loving ways and they have a terrific time.

Jack & Denise
The Voyeur Next Door

Our house has an inviting swimming pool right in the middle of our beautifully landscaped yard. We spend lots of time out there, but there's no escaping that we have some nosy neighbors. I've gotten to a place where I just ignore them. I don't care who sees what Denise and I are do when we're out there. Like last Saturday.

It was a warm, sunny, summer day and I had been out running errands. When I got home, Denise was in the yard relaxing in the Jacuzzi. She had her head back, her eyes closed, and she was wearing a very revealing leopard skin swimsuit – it barely covers her nipples and crotch. Denise is really comfortable with her body and knows how sexy she looks in her skimpy little suits. I think she was waiting for me, and what a beautiful sight she was when I looked out the window. I don't think she even heard me come in. So I put on my swim trunks and surprised her, tiptoeing out to the pool and sliding into the water without her even hearing me.

She opened her eyes just as I got close enough to give her a little kiss and a big hug. I told her she was a sight for sore eyes, and how lucky I was to have her waiting for me when I got home. The sun was sinking and a gentle breeze had started to blow. The warm water was just what I needed to relax after my hectic afternoon. I sat next to her and leaned my head back. I closed my eyes and felt all the day's stress float out of me.

Denise gave me a kiss on the cheek and sat on my lap. She arched her back and her beautiful breasts strained against her swimsuit. I couldn't resist stroking them. Denise asked if I noticed she had put on my favorite bathing suit. I said I noticed right away, and kissed her cute little belly button, which was exposed by the plunging neckline. Denise chuckled and nibbled on my ear. Then she gave it a harder bite. Ow! I turned her over and playfully spanked her bottom. I was in the mood for some fun this afternoon and Denise was happily going along with me.

She kissed me deeply, holding me tight. Then she stood and pulled me up with her. We hugged, and the cool breeze was refreshing against our wet skin. I was about to sink back down into the warm water when Denise surprised me by pulling my trunks off! She's not usually that aggressive and this was a stimulating surprise. I sat back on the edge of the Jacuzzi waiting to see what she had in mind. The sun felt warm and inviting on my skin. Denise rubbed her hands across my chest, sucking my nipples. She made her way downward, stroking and kissing my abs. Smiling up at me, she slowly placed my dick in her mouth. It felt amazing. The minute her warm lips and tongue touched my cock I was in heaven. I leaned back, savoring the moment.

Out of the corner of my eye, I saw movement. There was someone in the window next door. It was our neighbor, Emily, who has a knack for showing up at the window just as Denise and I are getting it on. I usually just ignore her.

I figure we're in our own yard, and if she enjoys watching, let her. It wasn't about to stop me now. But something was different that day... it was the first time I noticed her fondling herself as she watched.

I closed my eyes again, not wanting to be distracted from the pleasure Denise was giving me. She was cupping my balls in her hands while she sucked my dick. It was bliss, and the moment I shut my eyes I forgot about everything else. I felt like I was on fire as Denise worked me over. She slid my dick in and out, in and out of her warm wet mouth. I was only semi-erect, but it completely relaxed me... like I was floating away.

Denise kept stroking me and pushing me deeper and deeper into her mouth. Even though I wasn't getting hard, I told her what she was doing felt great. When I opened my eyes I saw a movement at the neighbor's window again. I whispered to Denise that Emily was watching us again... and I thought she was getting off on it because I saw her fondling herself. Denise chuckled. "Do ya think she'll like this?" she asked, with a devilish look on her face as she slowly licked my cock from the root to the tip, savoring every inch.

I smiled and told her she was a naughty girl. She licked all around my cock, covering every inch with her warm wet tongue. I could have drifted away again, but I kept my eyes open this time, watching Denise pleasure me. It looked so sexy. I felt like the luckiest guy in the world having this beautiful woman work me over! Part of me didn't ever want her to stop, but I had something else in mind.

I gently pulled Denise's head off my cock and lifted her up, sitting her on the edge of the Jacuzzi. She was already very turned on. She leaned back and closed her eyes. Her beautiful breasts popped out of her skimpy swimsuit, begging to be licked. I flicked her nipples with my tongue and sucked them into my mouth, taking turns from one to the other.

25

Denise moaned. I gently guided her down onto the deck and propped her legs on my shoulders. She knew what was coming and her breathing quickened. She sighed, running her hands through my hair. I planted soft kisses on her thighs and nipped at her pussy through her swimsuit. I felt her pulse quicken too. I teased her like that for a bit and let her anticipate. Then I gently pulled the swimsuit away from her pussy, paused for just a moment, and then stuck my tongue in deep for a taste.

Denise practically screamed. It must have felt as good as it tasted; it was delicious. I had to have more. I kissed her pussy all over and started sucking on it. Denise moaned again... she was blissed out. I flicked my tongue into her, faster and faster, putting more pressure on her clit. Denise went crazy. She was thrusting her pelvis up to meet my hungry mouth, driving me to devour her even more. The more I sucked and licked, the more intense her movements became, her body twisting from side to side. She clamped her legs around my head. Gasping for breath and then giggling, she grabbed my head and said she couldn't take much more... it was too good and it was driving her crazy! Her body was hyper-sensitive, tensing at the slightest touch.

But I knew now was not the time to stop. Denise was so close to coming. I rubbed her clit vigorously, licking and sucking her pussy with a passion. I don't know if it was the sun, or the water, or just being outside, but I was like a mad man. I couldn't get enough of my wife. She felt like the sexiest person on earth and we were in our own private Eden. I didn't want to let go of her.

I reached up and caressed her breast with one hand while I continued rubbing her clit with the other hand, my tongue flicking in and out of her the whole time. She was on the edge now and I was going to take her right over it. She rocked her pelvis up, thrusting uncontrollably, and I rocked right along with her rhythm.

I felt her tighten around my tongue. I knew she was about to come. She pressed my head down into her, clamping her legs around me. Her body responded to every move I made. Knowing how much pleasure she was feeling was a huge turn-on. I wanted to give her more and more. Denise held me tightly, my face jammed into her pussy. Her whole body stiffened and she let out a long, loud moan. She climaxed big... hard and long. Then her body went limp.

I released her and she laid there on the side of the pool, gasping for breath. I lay next to her, softly caressing her warm skin. Her breathing slowly returned to normal. She opened her eyes and rose up, smiling at me... a languid sexy half-smile. Her eyes were full of bliss. She reached over and returned my caress, telling me I was an amazing man and that I had made her feel awesome.

I lifted her down into the Jacuzzi and she wrapped her legs around my waist. I twirled her through the water. We kissed and hugged and sat down to bask in the bubbles. I felt warm and satisfied. Watching Denise enjoy herself so much and knowing I could take her to those heights was its own special kind of pleasure.

I loved bringing her to such a powerful orgasm with my tongue and fingers. It didn't matter that I didn't come... and it didn't matter who was watching. In fact, I wondered if my neighbor got even half the pleasure out of watching as we got out of doing! Even though I worked it, I remember it as one of the most relaxing afternoons I ever had.

~~~

"I like to be surprised. I like a woman with imagination... and very uninhibited... even kinky."

"I love it when Brenda totally plans out a sexy evening."

"I wish my girlfriend would surprise me with some sexual fantasy or escapade and just really take control."

For Kara, a lot of thought and creativity went into planning a special sexual surprise for her husband Michael...

Michael & Kara
Forbidden Fantasy

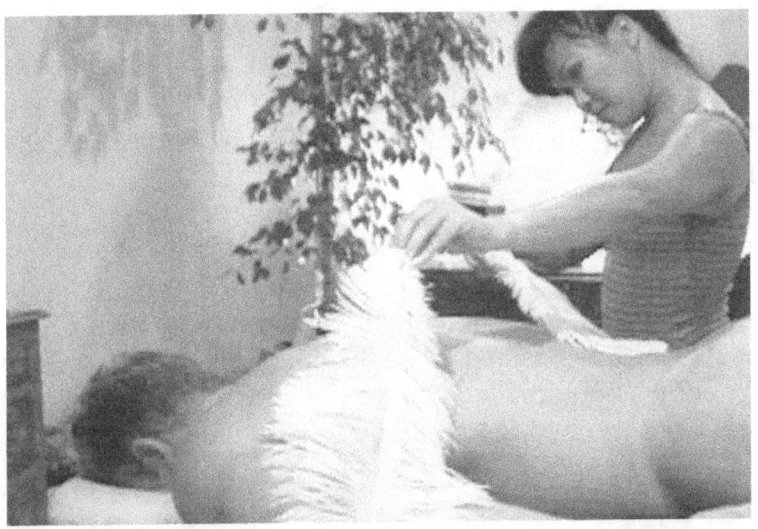

My wife Kara is full of surprises. Things can be going along on a nice comfortable routine, and suddenly she'll pull a rabbit out of the hat. My life with her is never boring, that's for sure. It adds a special zing to our relationship. She waits until I least expect it, then springs something completely new on me.

There is absolutely no way I could have guessed what she had planned for me last week. Wednesday evening is always our date night. We're both busy, so we make a point of putting everything else aside and making time for each other on Wednesdays. We take turns picking a movie or a favorite restaurant or sometimes just a long walk if the weather is nice. It keeps us close sharing our special Wednesdays every week and it's something we've both come to cherish.

When I headed home from work last week, I knew we would be going out but I didn't know where. It was Kara's turn to choose. I was looking forward to whatever our getaway was, just like always. I was hungry, and I was hoping she made reservations at a new restaurant we had talked about.

When I turned the key in the front door, Kara was standing there in the entryway, waiting to greet me. She had a big smile on her face and she looked terrific. She said hi, gave me a big kiss and asked me how my day was. I told her it was a lot better now that I was home with her. I wrapped my arms around her and teased her, asking where she was taking me for dinner that night and saying that they better have good food because I was hungry.

A mischievous smile played across Kara's face. She said she was pretty sure I'd like where she was taking me, and then she took my hand and led me through the living room. I kept questioning her, asking what the plan was, when were we leaving, was she driving or was I? She grinned, and pulling me toward the bedroom told me to be patient and just follow her.

Now, don't get me wrong, I'm happy to head to the bedroom with my wife anytime. But this was Wednesday. We were supposed to be going out, and I had been looking forward to it. But she looked so proud of herself that I played along. I asked her if she had another one of her surprises planned for me, and she nodded. I pressed her for details but she toyed with me, reminding me that if she told me it wouldn't be a surprise at all, would it? I was to hush and follow her.

She led me by the hand into the bedroom, but we didn't stop when we got there; she led me through and kept going. I must admit I was really curious at this point. The idea of a surprise is always stimulating, and it was already beginning to work on me. I followed her through the French doors and outside to our yard, where the pool area was lit with candles. Were we going swimming, I wondered? Not exactly what I would have chosen, but I was game if that's what she wanted to do. But she didn't stop at the pool either. She led me by the hand around the pool to the cabana in the back of the yard. She pulled back the curtain, and inside was an awesome surprise.

The cabana smelled of incense and glowed with warm candlelight. There was a massage table set up in the middle, and standing behind it was a beautiful Asian woman. Her gorgeous skin glowed in the candlelight. She wore a fragrant white flower behind her ear, highlighting her long wavy black hair. She wore a turquoise swimsuit that accented her shapely figure.

Wow! This was not what I expected in our backyard! The woman acknowledged me by sensuously stroking a long white ostrich feather across her chest. She wielded it with a flourish, beckoning to me to come forward.

I was speechless for a moment and trying to take it all in. I asked my wife Kara what this was all about. She grinned and said, "Happy Birthday, Baby." I was taken aback. It wasn't my birthday for a few more days and I thought we would be doing the usual cake-and-candles thing over the weekend. But I was definitely up for celebrating early, especially with this set-up. I felt like I was standing in the middle of a movie set. Kara had cast me as the star of this scene and I was ready for my role. Grinning from ear to ear I said, "Thank you Kara. This looks amazing."

She introduced me to Chandi, the masseuse, and told Chandi to take good care of her man. Then she walked away, leaving me alone with this gorgeous woman. I'm a typical hot-blooded male, and the first thought that flashed across my mind was that maybe I was in for a threesome.

At this point, I was in for the ride, wherever it took me. Chandi said she was ready to get started. She asked me to take off my clothes lay down on my stomach on the table. Okay, I figured, she's the boss. I'll do what I'm told and see where it goes. Knowing my wife had planned this scenario for me added an unusual spice to the mixture. A little shiver ran through me.

31

I was happy to obey Chandi, and was out of my clothes and stretched out on the table before her in a hot second. Chandi told me to close my eyes. She gently and slowly stroked the long white ostrich feather from my heels to my head. It tickled a little but felt wonderful. She used a soft touch and I could feel my muscles relaxing immediately. After covering the length of my body several times with the soft feathery strokes, she switched it up a bit. I wasn't sure what she was using now because I kept my eyes closed, but she replaced the feather for something a little more bristly. It too felt wonderful.

Chandi continued stroking up and down my body with three or four different textures, each one getting progressively rougher. Eventually she was stroking me with a brush that had a coarse surface like a small wide broom. She swept it along the length of my body and my skin tingled beneath it. It felt like she was sweeping all the day's stress right out of me. It was very stimulating. All the nerve endings on my skin were alive.

I exhaled, letting go of everything but this sensual feeling. Chandi moved on from the soft sweeping strokes. She rolled a pair of small wooden wheels over my muscles, applying gentle pressure that pushed the stress out of me. After she massaged up and down my back with the wooden wheels, she slowly and softly rubbed warm oil into my skin. I felt like I was melting. She rubbed and kneaded me from top to bottom, her touch very soothing. She was a superb masseuse; I felt my whole being become mellow and aware. The aroma of the incense was mild and the atmosphere was relaxing and invigorating at the same time.

Chandi's agile hands moved down from my back, deftly kneading my butt and thighs. As she worked on me, I felt a spark simmering between my legs… but I knew I had to control it, because just then Chandi had me roll over onto my back. She slowly coated the front side of my body with oil, working from my chest down to my feet. Her fingers rolled and kneaded my flesh until I felt like I was floating.

My dick was resting on my groin, and up to now had been on its best behavior. But Chandi put me to the test when she lifted it and rubbed oil over it. She held it gently but firmly, massaging it with the same expert technique she used on my muscles. It was too much for me, fueling the flames that were already flickering beneath the surface. I opened my eyes and watched Chandi stroking my dick, and I couldn't control my thoughts... I saw erotic images of making love to her.

I reached out and tested the waters, gently cupping her ass. Chandi placed my hand back on the massage table and softly said that I should save that for my wife. She gave me a knowing little smile. I knew she was right. I closed my eyes and she continued massaging me while I drifted off on a cloud of tranquility.

Moments later there was a change of pace. I felt another pair of hands get in on the action. Kara had joined us again, massaging my chest while Chandi worked on my thighs. It was highly erotic having two beautiful women center their concentration on making my body feel great. I was one lucky man! Kara slid her hands down my chest and slowly stroked my abs, moving lower and lower until she was massaging between my legs. This time there was no controlling the energy surge that shot down my body... my wife knew exactly how I liked it.

Kara smiled and asked me if I liked my present. How could I not? I told her it was wonderful and that this might be my best birthday present ever. She said I deserved something special and was glad to see me so relaxed. She wanted me to lay back and enjoy it.

She started stroking my dick, her soft hands sliding along my

33

oiled skin. I reached up and pulled the strap of her negligee down off her shoulder. Her voluptuous breast bounced out and more than filled my hand. I played with her nipple, feeling it become erect between my fingers. I don't remember seeing Chandi leave, but Kara and I were alone now. She stripped off her negligee, leaned over me and sucked my dick into her mouth. Kara knows that watching her savor me makes me want to get between her legs, and tonight was no exception.

I tried to control myself as she sucked it in, took it out, licked it and kissed the tip. I was growing harder by the minute and dying to make passionate love to my wife. I asked her if I could have some dessert. She said I could have whatever I wanted, and suggested we move out to the Jacuzzi. I rose up from the massage table, suddenly feeling energized, and pulled her close. I rubbed my dick between Kara's legs and she responded by placing my hand back on her warm breast. She kissed me deeply, and gazing in my eyes wished me a happy birthday.

She took my hand and led me out to the Jacuzzi. I stepped down into the water and Kara followed. Turning her back to me she leaned over, slowly sliding onto my hard and ready dick. I spanked her butt and thrust into her. It felt incredible, and she wiggled her butt at me, letting me know she liked it and wanted more. I gave her another gentle slap, and each time I spanked her bottom she tightened her pussy around my dick. She was tight as a drum and keeping rhythm on me with her own sexy beat.

I bent forward over her butt and reached around to massage her clit. Kara was quivering. I was so worked up from the massage that I knew I wouldn't last long. Every bone in my body was engaged and every nerve was tingling. The smell of the incense-filled cabana, the sensuous touch of the feathers, and the sight of my beautiful wife joining in to massage me all filled my head. I heard Kara's moans and

34

kissed her soft sweet skin, tasting her desire. All my senses were full and ready to burst.

My climax was as sharp and strong as a cymbal crash. My body tensed against Kara, spent by the unexpected sexual sweetness of the evening.

Kara and I slowly slid back into the warm, bubbling water. I kissed her deeply, in love and appreciation. I told her I'd always remember this as one of my all-time best birthday celebrations.

~~~

Ask ten men what's attractive in a woman, and you'll get ten different answers...

"White t-shirt and jeans. That's sexy."

"I'm definitely a leg man. I love legs."

"I tend to like women with dark hair and dark eyes... "

"Face, skin, but mostly eyes. Eyes and lips, I guess."

"It's physical attractiveness to begin with... but ultimately a woman who is uninhibited keeps me interested."

"To me, it's an incredible turn-on to watch my wife masturbate. But I honestly don't know if she likes to watch me, too."

"It could be awkward at first. But it might be exciting.... something to try."

Carl tells how much he enjoyed it when his girlfriend felt comfortable enough to let him watch…

Carl & Bianca
Private Passion

On Saturday mornings Bianca and I like to get up early and go for long walks on the beach. We walk at least 4 miles and sometimes we even jog a little. It's a peaceful time and we never feel compelled to experience the walk as a routine. We like to mix it up. Sometimes we talk a lot, and sometimes we just walk and hold hands or sit and watch the waves. Afterward, I usually make a big breakfast while Bianca takes a shower. This particular Saturday was a little different.

When we got back to the house, my lady immediately took off her clothes and headed for the shower. I wanted to get comfortable before I hit the kitchen and made breakfast, so I undressed and put on my robe. The bathroom was already nice and steamy when I walked in to ask Bianca if she wanted a cup of coffee.

She was basking under the new shower head I had installed that makes you feel like you're standing under a waterfall. She looked like a beautiful island princess. Her silky black hair was dripping wet and her long lean body glistened in the water. She had her eyes closed, and was rubbing her hands across her tight little breasts, squeezing them so that her nipples stood erect. It was a beautiful sight. As I stood there watching her, I realized my crotch was throbbing. Breakfast could wait... I sat down to enjoy the show for a few minutes.

My robe fell open, and my dick poked through, standing at attention. Instinctively, I began to stroke myself. When Bianca opened her eyes and saw me, she teasingly asked if I was enjoying watching her, as she slid her hand down between her legs. I didn't have to say anything... my dick answered by popping up even higher.

Bianca smiled and continued stroking herself under the flowing water. She told me in a sultry voice that she was going to show me what she liked to do sometimes in the shower. She stuck her finger in her mouth, pulled it out and asked if I knew what was coming next. I continued to stroke myself, responding "No... why don't you show me."

Bianca grabbed the shower gel and slathered it all over her breasts. She worked up lots of creamy lather and rubbed it over her abs and down between her legs. She caressed her thighs one by one. Then she turned around and bent over, smoothing the lather over her beautiful round butt cheeks. She held her hand out under the stream of water, rinsing off the lather, and then slid her finger into her pussy. She began to sway like a sultry hula girl, slowly swinging her hips back and forth under the water as she pleasured herself. The stream washed away the bubbles as she rocked beneath it, playfully bumping and grinding her ass toward the shower door, tempting me with her beautiful body and glowing skin.

Her eyes were closed and she was in her own world. She tweaked her nipples and slid her finger down to massage her clit. Moaning, she leaned against the wall of the shower and slid down to the floor. She bent her knees and spread her

37

legs wide open so I could watch everything she did. Her finger pumped in and out and then moved up to massage her clit. Back and forth she caressed herself, from her G-spot to her clit. I knew she was lost in her pleasure zone when she arched her back, because I know her body so well. She looked over at me, smiled coyly and asked if I would hand her the lube and her shower brush.

I was happy to comply. I picked up the lube and squirted some into my own palm before I passed it to her along with her brush. My cock was bone hard and the slippery smooth lube felt great. I wasn't sure how long I could last before erupting. I slowed my strokes, not wanting to miss one moment of the show Bianca was putting on for me. She rubbed the lube onto her clit and all along the folds of her pussy, and then spread it all over the handle of her shower brush.

Then she turned it on. That was a surprise! I had no idea the thing was also a vibrator. She slid the handle inside her pussy and touched the tip of her clit. I could tell by the look in her eyes that she was no longer conscious of my presence. She was absorbed in the pleasure she was giving herself. Her body was on automatic pilot. She knew exactly how to touch herself and each stroke brought greater pleasure. When she focused on me and told me how good it felt, I couldn't hold back. I had been stroking myself faster and faster as I watched her, and when she included me in her pleasure I went over the edge. I closed my eyes and exploded into my hand.

When I looked back at Bianca, the handle of the vibrator was half way up her pussy. She slowly pumped it in and out as she massaged her clit. Each time she pushed the handle in, it went a little deeper. When she was about to climax, she opened her legs wide, pulled out the vibrator and laid it on her clit, grinding her pelvis into it. She clenched her teeth almost as if she were in pain and threw her head back. Then she clamped her legs tight around the handle and her hand.

38

I could tell she was coming… her body was trembling as the waves of pleasure shot through her.

When she finally went limp, I stepped into the shower and picked her up. She opened her eyes, smiled and gave me a deep passionate kiss. I had never seen Bianca masturbate before, and it was quite an experience. She had to have a lot of trust in me to let me watch her be so vulnerable, and that was as much of a turn-on as any physical act.

~~~

"I like it when she talks dirty to me."

"I have heard stories and told stories before sex that's sort of a prelude, or perhaps that'll even initiate the sex… just talking about this or that, or what other people have done or what we have done in the past."

"I like it when Nancy tells me sexy stories while we make love."

Here's how it went for Jay and Sofia…

Jay & Sofia
Love at Sea

For me, the difference between good sex and great sex comes from little things... the extra stuff that adds spice. Anytime I have sex, I enjoy myself, but it's even more enjoyable when my wife talks to me during sex. Sometimes I like her to talk dirty. Other times, I like her to take me into one of her fantasies, or talk about what she wants to do with me. Last time we made love, she told me a great story.

Sofia and I were already making love when I reminded her how much I loved her active imagination. I asked her to tell me a story. She paused for a minute and said she'd be happy to tell me a story... did I want her to make something up? Or tell me a true story? I slowed my strokes and pondered for a moment. There was something arousing about listening to an erotic story of something she'd actually done. I wanted a true story tonight.

She said she could tell me about something that happened a long time ago, before she met me, when she made love up in the lookout of a boat.

40

She said she thought it was a really sexy story, but since it was about her with another man, she wanted me to be sure I was comfortable hearing it. I appreciated her laying it out like that for me. I hesitated, but my curiosity was already piqued. I think she knew that. I thanked her for asking and assured her it was okay. I was all ears.

So Sofia launched into her story:

"It happened a few years ago... I was invited to a party on a friend's boat called the Lazy Daisy. It was a beautiful boat with three bedrooms, a living room, the galley dining area and the lookout, which was up above everything else. A group of us were in the living room hanging out and having a good time. The music, food and drinks were great."

"My date, David, and I stepped outside for some evening air and walked around the deck looking for a quiet place to talk. As I leaned on the boat's railing, gazing over the cityscape across the water, David put his arms around me. He was in a randy mood, and I felt him harden as he cuddled against me. I began to get aroused too. He squeezed me tighter and asked if I'd like to go up to the lookout with him. He said the view was fantastic up there. It sounded like a fun idea."

"David helped me up onto the first rung of the ladder that led up to the lookout. As I began to climb, the wind caught my dress and blew it up above my waist... and I was wearing a very skimpy thong. I smoothed the skirt back down but the wind kept blowing it up again. David was climbing behind me, and suddenly his lips were brushing against the cheek of my butt. He teased that we might not need to climb all the way to the top, because he was enjoying the view already. We both laughed, and he joined me on my rung of the ladder, pressing his body into me. He caressed me and smoothed my skirt back down into place."

"We slowly and carefully continued climbing to the top and stepped up into the lookout. It was a clear night and David was right... the view was spectacular. He pulled me into his arms and kissed me. I felt warm and wonderful. I leaned over the railing, looking out over the water and the city lights in the distance. David was behind me, nuzzling his face into my hair. He reached around and cupped my breasts, massaging them as his breath quickened. Then he very gently pulled up the sides of my dress".

"The cold air tingled but his fingers sliding under my thong were warm. My mind said to resist. After all, there were other people on board. But my body didn't want him to stop. I opened my legs and let him in. I was already wet from his body pressing against me and his warm breath on the nape of my neck. I reached back and held onto his tight thighs. He sighed, and my hands traveled forward, massaging his groin."

"He said he wanted to be in me. I was already turned on, and when he whispered that in my ear, I knew I wanted it too. I unzipped his pants and freed his cock, which was rock hard. He moaned at the touch of my hands. I leaned over on the railing, and he pulled my thong aside, exposing my pussy."

"Very gently, he slid into my moist folds. He moved the tip of his cock up and down along the wetness and my heart started to flutter. I felt like a flower opening its petals to receive him. He thrust into me and I closed my eyes, feeling the salty ocean mist kiss my cheeks. He was intense. His passion was fierce and it sent waves of pleasure through me. He gripped me tighter, pulling me back and pushing himself into me again and again. I knew he was going to come right away."

"He held my hips against him and exploded into me. It was fast and hot. It left me trembling, and for a moment I lost all space and time. The water swirled around me and the stars seemed brighter than ever."

"It was the first time I ever had sex outdoors, so it was a unique experience. David leaned against me, gasping for breath. I felt beautiful and sexy with him holding me that way."

"After he recovered, he kissed me tenderly and held me close. We stayed up there in the lookout for a few minutes, catching our breath and basking in the starlight. It was a special night that I will never forget. The End."

When Sofia finished her story, I was totally turned on. Listening to her talk, I had pictured the events unfolding, and I wanted to hear more. I asked her to show me exactly how she kissed David. Sofia hesitated. Again, she wanted to make sure I was okay with all this, because she didn't want to continue if it would cause any problem between us. She's really smart that way, and would never do anything to harm our relationship. I kissed her and looked into her eyes, assuring her I was enjoying it.

So she went with it. She said she'd show me how they kissed, then pulled me to her, kissing me tenderly, while sucking and nibbling on my lips. Suddenly she thrust her tongue deep into my mouth. She took my hand and slid it to her breast. She sucked on my lip some more, then pushed my head to her breast. I sucked on her nipples, first one then the other, and she moaned with pleasure.

There was something so hot about it. Picturing Sofia with another man - and knowing she was all mine now - was unusually erotic. The combination of her story and her beautiful body there in bed with me was very arousing. So I pressed for more. I asked her to tell me again what happened after they kissed. She said they made love doggy style while she leaned over the railing... that the lights on shore were sparkling... and the boat was rocking... and they were rocking right along with it. "Did it feel like this, baby?" I asked, thrusting into her from behind.

43

She gasped at the sudden action. I felt her pussy get wetter as she moaned and kept repeating, "Oh yeah… just like that."

I whispered that I wanted her to keep going. I wanted her to give me details of exactly what happened next. She could hardly catch her breath, but she continued, telling me how he lifted her into the lookout chair and pulled her dress up over her head. Her breasts were exposed and his eyes lit up at the sight. He told her they were beautiful, and he couldn't resist them. He greedily sucked a nipple into his mouth like he was a baby. Then his big warm hands caressed her body and he worked his way down to her pussy. She said she was wet and ready for him, and that when he touched her he joked that he'd found a hidden treasure. The boat listed, and after they regained their balance, he lifted her legs, hooked them over the arms of the chair, and knelt down in front of her.

"Did he do it like this, baby?" I asked Sofia, as I spread her legs and moved my finger to her clit, rubbing gently. She sighed and said yes, but he didn't feel as good as I did. That was what I wanted to hear. She said he dived between her legs and licked her like it was his last meal. I grinned, licking her stomach and moving downward, understanding what she wanted. I thrust my tongue deep into her and savored her like never before. Her whole body was quivering, responding to my touch. She moaned with pleasure. I was getting harder by the minute, and suddenly couldn't resist the urge to be inside her. I had to have her, right then. Climbing on top of her, I rubbed the tip of my cock on her clit and slid into her as she gasped for breath, trying to continue her story.

She closed her eyes and said she remembered looking at his big cock and thinking she wanted more. So she stood up and pushed him into the chair, climbed on top of him and gently slid down onto him. She said she moved real slowly at first, up and down, up and down, teasing him… until he begged her to go faster.

Sofia was lost in her story. For a moment I wondered if she wished she were back there again. Then she whispered that I felt incredibly good to her, and it confirmed she was still right here in the moment with me. It made me even hotter.

I prompted her to tell me what happened next, pumping in and out as I held her tight. She said she was feeling so free with the breeze blowing through her hair, riding his cock like she was a cowgirl riding a pony, and loving every minute of it. When he came inside her, she could feel his heat. The boat was rocking and they were rocking each other hard right along with it.

"Like this?" I asked again, rocking into her with all my might. She gasped and said yeah, just like that. We were embraced in sexual frenzy, and I felt a charge ripple through her pussy and back up through my cock. Sofia gripped me and squealed, and my body stiffened. Her pussy throbbed with contractions and I climaxed hard. We were in total sync, and I hurtled into it, pushing us both over the top.

Sofia and I laid there in each other's arms for a long spell before either of us spoke. Then she softly asked if I was okay. Was I okay with her telling me that story?

"Are you kidding?" I answered, "That was the best bedtime story I ever heard."

~~~

"I think it would be exciting to try some mild dominance and bondage sort of thing... to tie up my partner with handcuffs or maybe rope and to have my way with her for a while. And it might even be exciting to do it the other way around... to give up that power would be very exciting. I'd be very vulnerable, of course. And that could be a big turn-on."

"Sometimes, I like to take complete control. And I like when she complies."

Dan and his wife Heather sometimes toy with submission in their lovemaking...

Dan & Heather
Blindfolds and Cherries

Every year my wife Heather and I take a ski trip to Tahoe with some friends. This year the snow was better than ever, which was great, because I love to ski all day. It's a real romantic setting and when the skiing is over for the day I look forward to spending time with Heather snuggled up in our cozy chalet. She likes to ski with the other women on the intermediate slopes while we men go for the maximum thrill, so at the end of the day when we're cold and tired, we really look forward to being together.

On our first day there we had both spent hours on the slopes. By the time I got back to our chalet, I was tired but exhilarated at the same time. I had spent hours going for it full tilt, and had worked all the stress of the workweek out of my body.

The sun was bright and the snow was crisp and it had been a great start to our vacation.

Heather was already back from the slopes and enjoying a cup of cocoa when I walked into our chalet.

As I got out of my cold damp ski clothes, I told her all about the trails we had discovered and the hills we had skied. I was chilled to the bone and couldn't wait to take a hot shower. When I was done, Heather was waiting for me with a hug, a kiss, and a cup of frothy hot cocoa. I was invigorated from skiing. Even though my muscles would feel it in the morning, right now I was still charged up and feeling no pain. And I was feeling randy.

I wanted to play "9 1/2 Weeks", our own version of an erotic movie that came out in 1986. We love the DVD, and in our favorite scene, Mickey Rourke blindfolds Kim Basinger and feeds her strawberries and other treats. We hadn't done that for a long time, so it didn't take much persuading when I suggested it to Heather.

At first she gave me a devilish smile and said she wasn't really in the mood… and I'd have to talk her into it. I unraveled the scarf from her neck and tied it gently around her eyes as a blindfold. I asked if that helped to get her in the mood and she giggled. She said she wasn't completely convinced yet that she wanted to play, so I took her by the hand and carefully led her to the center of the kitchen.

I laid her on the floor and untied her robe, exposing her beautiful body. I couldn't resist caressing her, feeling her curves and stroking her soft skin before removing her lacy bra. Her nipples looked like little cherries sitting on a mound of inviting ice cream. I sucked one into my mouth and nibbled at it until she started to squirm. She smiled and said I was very good at coaxing.

I reached up to the counter for a chocolate-covered cherry and rubbed it around her nipple. I asked her to guess what it was but she had no idea. I told her to pay close attention as I broke open the cherry and let the juice drip over her nipples. I licked the sweet juice from her breast and used the cherry to massage her other nipple. The cool air on her body made her nipples erect. She moaned as I sucked on one and then the other.

She reached to pull me into her but I pushed her hands back to the sides of her body. "Not yet," I said. First I wanted her to guess what I was rubbing on her. I moved my lips to her nose so she could smell the confection She guessed right away... probably because we didn't have much stocked in the cabin that had the sticky sweet aroma of both fruit and chocolate!

Next I opened a honey bear and drizzled it from her nipples all the way down her chest to her belly button. She laughed at the gooey sensation and said she wasn't sure she liked the way whatever it was felt. When I licked and sucked the honey from her nipples and followed the sweet trail down to her belly button, she changed her mind. She definitely liked the way *that* felt.

I slid back up to her lips and gave her a sweet honey kiss. Then I opened a bottle of chocolate syrup and squeezed a circle around her nipple. It was chilly against her skin and she shivered. I licked her nipple again, lapping up the chocolate. She said I was warming her up, and I knew she meant in more ways than one. I slid up and kissed her with my chocolate-covered lips. She smiled and called me a very sweet guy... sweet and chocolate-y. It was starting to get messy, but we were both having fun.

Next I held a strawberry over her chest and drizzled chocolate over its ripe redness. When I delivered this sweet treat to her lips, she hungrily nibbled at it and licked her lips, savoring my delectable concoction. I prepared another chocolate-covered strawberry and fed it to her, telling her she was getting seconds for being such a good girl.

Next I took an orange slice and teased her with it. I rubbed it on her lips without letting her really taste it. Every time she tried to lick or nibble it, I pulled it away. I prodded her to guess what it was. She thought a minute and tentatively asked if it was a slice of grapefruit. I told her that was a very good guess, but she'd have to try again. I brushed the orange against her lips again and this time she got it right.

Next move, I made a glass of ice water and jiggled it next to her ear, the cubes gently clinking in the glass. She feigned dread, talking about how cold it was outside and saying she wasn't ready for that... couldn't I come up with something else? Without responding, I took a piece of ice and rubbed it over her lips, chin and down her neck. Immediately, goose bumps appeared on her skin, and she squealed, but she didn't object. I let a drop of water from the ice cube drip onto her lips and into her mouth. Then I held the cube in my teeth, pushing it slowly in and out of her mouth.

Heather responded with a little groan, enjoying the sensation and sucking on the ice. Moving down to her breasts, I circled her nipples with the cube. Continuing down to her stomach and belly button, I let the ice cube travel all over her body and back up to my favorite place again...her nipples.

She shivered and giggled that it was too cold. I rubbed my hand over her stomach, warming her up a bit, and then gently slid her panties off. I traced a line with the ice cube from her abdomen to her thighs and over her bush. Pausing, I slid the ice cube over her clit and then slowly pushed it down into her pussy. Her whole body shivered but she didn't complain.

Looking at her lying there, fully exposed to me, was very arousing. I forgot about the food and the game. I was hot for my wife and wanted to take her right now.

The thought of fire and ice intrigued me as I slid into her pussy, probing to find the ice cube. When I hit it, the cold sensation sent shivers through my body and made my dick even harder. The sweet, the cold, my blindfolded wife laying there under me... it was all very exciting.

I began to pump and thrust with abandon. Heather responded intensely. She grabbed my thighs and pulled me in deeper, something she only does when she's really turned on. Her supple body was gripping my dick so hard that I was like a time bomb ready to explode... and then boom! I burst into her as she held me tightly against her.

After a moment, she smiled and took off the blindfold, telling me what great fun it had been. I gazed into her lovely eyes, no longer hidden behind the blindfold. I kissed her lips, then her eye lids, and told her how much I loved her.

~~~

Ted and Beverley, who work out together, end up creating a very special personal routine...

Ted & Beverley
Private Trainer

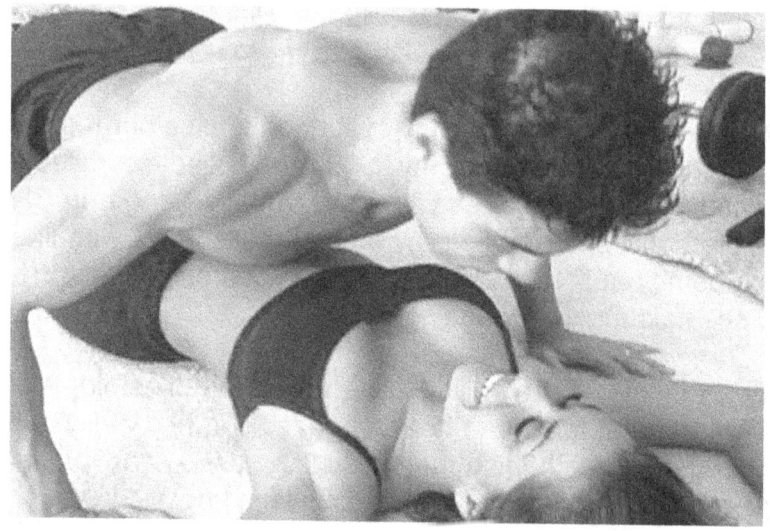

I love to exercise; it makes me feel good about myself. I've converted one room of my house into a mini gym and I make pretty good use of it. More and more, my girlfriend Beverley and I have been working out there together. She seems to especially enjoy it when I push her a little bit, putting her through her paces and trying to motivate her to do better. She calls me her "very private" personal trainer.

I've always known Beverley is inventive, but I had no idea just how creative she could be – especially when it comes to amorous pursuits. The last time I trained her, she showed me a trick or two when she led me through a very motivating mix of exercise and pleasure.

I had created a routine for us that we did several times a week. It utilized a full series of exercises so we'd be sure to work out both our upper and lower bodies. We'd usually warm up on the treadmill for about 10 minutes to get our hearts pumping, stretch to get the muscles ready, and then move on to the various machines. It's a good 45-minute workout.

The last time we went through the routine, Beverley and I first worked up a good sweat as usual. We hit the treadmill, did some stretching, and then moved to the rowing machine. Next we wanted to try out our new tension bar. To use it, you put a hand on each end of the flexible bar and pull the ends together. Beverley didn't have enough strength to do it correctly, so I stood behind her and helped her pull.

I have to admit that as serious as I am about exercising, I do lose my focus and get a little horny sometimes watching her work out. So it wasn't a big surprise that each time we pulled down on the bar my penis popped up and bumped her butt. She would laugh each time. After 10 reps, I suggested we move on to something else because Beverley was getting the giggles.

I took off my shirt and wiped the sweat from my upper body. Beverley walked over and stood in front of me with a nasty grin on her face. Out of nowhere, she leaned over and pulled my shorts down! "What are you doing?" I blurted out. She didn't answer; she just pushed me onto the rowing machine. Without saying a word she straddled the machine, bent over and kissed me.

I grabbed her ass and slid my hands up under her shorts. As soon as I touched the warmth there I pulled them off. She stopped kissing me and took her top off. Wow... exercise was taking on a whole new perspective. I could feel myself getting hard. I stroked myself with one hand and between Beverley's legs with the other. It was getting real juicy down there as she kissed me passionately. All of a sudden she stopped, stood up, and took hold of my cock. She said she had some inner muscles that I had been ignoring, and she wanted to work on strengthening them. Before I knew it, she was sliding down onto me.

I agreed that she had some mean muscles begging for my

53

attention. Leaning back, I used the sliding seat on the rowing machine to push myself further into her. Man, it felt so good. I kept rowing and she pumped back and forth with me. I knew Beverley was enjoying herself because her kisses got more intense. She was breathing deeply, and suddenly she was thrusting faster. The sound of our skin slapping together each time our bodies collided made me even hornier.

Beverley was panting now and I knew I was about to hit her spot. I told her how sexy she was as I kept pumping. She just moaned... she was off in her zone.

It was a very strange sensation... our muscles were already primed and we were pretty tired, but suddenly we were both energized again. There was no stopping it now. The contractions inside her gripped me, and I knew she was about to come. The thought put me over the edge. Beverley grabbed my arms and squeezed, and I couldn't hold out any longer. I came like a geyser blowing full steam. It was incredible. We kissed each other and laid back to rest.

I was blissed out, lying there and savoring the awesome experience. But we weren't done yet. Beverley was still feeling naughty, and she had a seductive plan in mind. She still had energy and said she wanted to work on her abs before we called it quits.

She lay on the mat and stretched. Sticking her feet under me for support, she started doing crunches in a slow and languid manner. Her form was great, as usual. With her hands behind her head she raised her shoulders up off the floor, holding the position for three seconds. One, two, three... I started counting her reps in my head, as any good trainer would do. Keep in mind that Beverley was still naked and I was sitting in front of her bent knees, so I had a pretty sexy view.

I surprised myself when I started getting turned on again so soon. Watching her crunching, up and down, up and down, I got fixated on her beautiful pussy. I'm pretty sure she knew exactly what she was doing to me! I suddenly wanted to taste her so bad! She finished up two sets of 15 crunches, and her abs looked tight and damn sexy. She paused to rest, letting her legs fall open. I couldn't resist planting a kiss on one of her soft thighs.

Of course, one kiss led to another and before I knew it her scent was intoxicating me. I brushed against her savory lips with my nose and mouth. Then I began probing her with my finger, sliding in and out and circling her clit. I moved over to her other thigh, softly planting kisses there, but Beverley's movements made it clear she wanted my attention back on her pussy. That really turned me on. I hesitated for a moment, teasing her while I enjoyed the view, and then stuck my tongue in for a taste.

One taste was all it took to get me licking and sucking. Beverley likes it when I nibble on her clit, so I nipped and nibbled until I worked her up into a frenzy. She clamped her hands on my head and pushed me deeper into her. The combination of her scent and her taste was intoxicating. I pushed my tongue down deep inside. Then I pressed against her clit, applying pressure with my tongue. Beverley was thrusting her hips, telling me she couldn't take any more. But she sure wasn't pushing me away!

Her juices were flowing and I was licking her like mad. I sucked and nibbled her clit while my finger dove deep inside her... in and out... in and out... I was mad with passion. Suddenly she arched her back and let out a wail. I knew I had hit her spot. Her whole body tensed and she came again, the lips of her pussy throbbing against my hungry mouth. When I knew she had had enough, I let her go and she collapsed back onto the gym mat. Then she relaxed. We lie there, worked out, worked over, and exhausted.

It didn't seem to matter anymore that I hadn't finished my routine. But after a few minutes, I forced myself up and stepped onto the treadmill. I thought if I could get up the energy, I'd do a short 10-minute jog and call it a day. But Beverley was still feeling devilish. I can't believe that girl's stamina. She stepped in front of me, bent down, grabbed my cock and began to stroke it until I was sticking straight out like a flagpole again.

She smiled and said that every part of our bodies was going to get a workout today... she had come hard, and it was my turn now. She licked the tip of my cock, teasing me, and started counting in a very seductive voice, sucking my cock in and out of her mouth with each number. That girl really knows how to treat my cock... stroking, sucking, and licking like there's no tomorrow. Watching her work on my cock and seeing how much she loves doing it is a huge turn-on.

All I could do was practice deep breathing and hold on tightly to the rail of the treadmill. I closed my eyes, growling and moaning as the waves of pleasure rippled through my body. Beverley could tell I was about to come again, so she gently slid my cock out of her mouth. She jumped off the treadmill and teased that she wouldn't want to interfere with my work-out.

She left me standing there and picked up the dumbbells. She got on her knees in front of a pillow-covered ottoman. Leaning over, she rested her chest on the pillows. Wow, she was naked and curvy and looked very appealing, even though I had thought I was spent. She was doing arm lifts with the weights but my mind was definitely on sex again.

She looked delicious laying over that cushion with her butt pointed straight up at me. I was standing there naked, staring at her backside and lost in the wonder of it. When I looked back down at myself, I was hard as a rock again.

That girl can really get me excited. I was getting thicker and stiffer as I watched her butt pumping in time to the arm lifts.

I hopped off the treadmill and knelt over her backside, doing push-ups right over her body. Each time I came down I would kiss one of her cheeks. It didn't last long because Beverley looked so tender I couldn't resist slipping my cock between her soft folds. She laughed and said it was definitely the best time she'd ever had exercising. By now I was riding her backside pretty good. I slipped out, massaging her clit and her juicy lips with the tip of my cock. She grabbed my leg and pulled me back in, telling me to do it harder.

I shifted my position and gripped the ottoman, doing push-ups right into her juicy opening. Beverley was pushing her butt into me, harder and harder, and it wasn't long before we both came, bursting from the effort. Her pussy contracted, sending wave after wave of pleasure through both our bodies until we collapsed onto each other.

My heart was beating fast and I had certainly worked up a sweat. After a few minutes, I said that strictly speaking as her trainer, I thought we had had an exceptional cardio workout. Beverley nodded, her eyes closed, and gave me a kiss.

~~~

"I love lingerie. I mean, I love garter belts and silk stockings and fishnet stockings. The more elaborate the better. It's like nice packaging on a beautiful gift."

"Lingerie is very sexy to me. The only bad thing about it is that it usually doesn't stay on very long!"

In the next story, Margo has a knack for putting on the kind of fashion show her man loves...

Matthew & Margo

Lacy Temptation

One of the things I really like about my wife, Margo, is she knows how much I can get turned on by what she wears. I never know exactly what she might come up with to pique my interest, but when she's in the mood, I get a fashion show that would make any man jealous. At this point she knows what kind of clothing turns me on the most... she knows my taste. And she's really good at adding things to her wardrobe that she knows I'll like. She loves indulging me... she doesn't even mind if I point out clothing that I like on other women.

One unforgettable evening when I arrived home, Margo was waiting to greet me at the door. She was wearing high heels, a lacy blouse, bra, garter belt, stockings and a big smile. She greeted me with a juicy passionate kiss. Talk about making a weary man come back to life! A surge of energy returned to my body. She took my hand and told me to follow her... she had a special night planned.

She led me into the living room, where the fireplace was crackling and the flickering flames cast a warm glow.

She motioned for me to sit down in my favorite chair. Removing my shoes, she loosened my tie and handed me a martini. I was in 1950's heaven.

Margo wanted me to enjoy my drink and get ready for a little show, because she had picked up a few new things on a shopping spree and wanted to model them. I pulled her into my lap and told her I liked what she had on now just fine. I wrapped my arms around her waist and nuzzled the flesh atop her soft breasts. She stood up and twirled for me. She looked delicious... I didn't know what we were having for dinner that night, but I wanted to have her for dessert.

As she bent over to sit back down on my knee, I realized she didn't have on any panties. I gently slid my fingers between her legs and caressed her soft white thighs. Leaning into her breasts, I kissed them softly. She took me under the chin and raised my head up, smiling and telling me to slow down. She was just getting started and there was a lot more to see.

She strolled off to the bedroom and left me there for a few minutes with my imagination running wild. I think that was part of her plan. Before I even saw her in her next outfit, I was imagining about ten of my own creations, each looking incredible on her and sexier than the one before.

Margo returned wearing a red strapless teddy. Her breasts were spilling out the top and about to bust free any moment. Nothing but a lacy ruffle hid them from view. The legs were high-cut up to there, exposing her all the way to her waist. It made her thighs look extra curvy and inviting. I wanted to dive into them then and there. But before I could get to her, she turned around and presented her soft round butt to me. Oh my goodness, the teddy was also a thong!

I reached for her and tried to pull her onto my lap. I wanted to feel that luscious booty on me. But she stepped away and flashed her tits at me before turning around again so I could at least cup that voluptuous booty. I licked my lips. Yum, yum. She was looking mighty tasty.

I loved the silky feel of the fabric when I rubbed my hands along the teddy. And I loved feeling Margo's lovely curves underneath. I squeezed her breasts and she pulled them away. She cupped them, fondling herself just out of my reach, saying they were all hers tonight. What a tease! She pulled the top down and leaned forward, presenting me with a soft breast and beautiful pink nipple. She said it was okay to touch now, as long as she could watch.

I stuck out my tongue, licked her nipple and sucked it into my mouth. She began to moan. She raised her legs and wrapped them around my waist. I caressed the soft supple skin on her butt and traveled down between her legs. My fingers slipped into her juicy pussy. The more I sucked her nipples, the wetter her pussy became. My dick was getting really hard and I was ready to do the wild thing. But Margo made me wait again. She said there was more to come, and pulled away from me, headed back for the bedroom.

Once again my mind started racing. I was really turned on and knew I couldn't wait much longer to get my hands on her again. Just when I was about to get up and join her in the bedroom, she strutted back toward me wearing a full-length black gown that was sheer on the bottom. The low-cut top accentuated her breasts and was pulled in snug around the middle.

The skirt had a slit in the front that shot all the way up to her tiny waist. She spun around and the sheer fabric billowed out around her like a wispy black cloud. Twirling until she was right in front of me, she asked if I wanted to see more. Then she flipped open the dress to reveal her naked bush. It was such a lovely sight I could hardly stay in my chair.

She's such a tease! She swayed her hips suggestively and ran her hand down to the slit in the dress. She caressed her thighs and ran her hands up over her butt until I couldn't stand it any more. Finally, she let me touch her.

She sat on my lap and proceeded to give me a very sexy lap dance. She was rubbing and grinding her butt into my groin and she knew she was setting me on fire. She rubbged her fingers on her clit and then stuck them in my mouth, knowing how much I dig her taste.

My groin was aching. I couldn't take much more of this because I knew I was about to burst. But she wasn't done teasing me. She kissed me and asked if I liked her new negligee. I nodded and told her I loved it, and she looked so sexy in it that maybe she should wear it all the time.

Margo giggled and slid off my lap and onto her knees, right in front of my crotch. She began to massage my groin, then unzipped me and stroked my dick. That was it for me... I couldn't wait another moment. Her fashion show was driving me wild, and I had to have her.

I picked her up and laid her on the couch. Ripping off my pants I dove on top of her and plunged deep inside. She squealed with the first thrust and pulled me tight.

We had a pretty incredible lovemaking session that night. And it was a cool switch-up being arroused by watching her get her clothes *on*, instead of *off*.

~~~

Trey and Jade experience an encounter with a common fantasy element that many couples enjoy acting out...

Trey & Jade

Sex and Strangers

My best friend figures into this fantasy. His name is Tiger. He's my dog. It started when I was taking Tiger out for his daily walk in the park one day last weekend. It was a beautiful afternoon, and we both needed the exercise, so we took a little jog.

Tiger is pretty much a little ball of fluff, but he's a feisty one. We had just finished our jog and were slowing down to head home when we rounded a corner and almost ran right into the biggest dog I've ever seen. My "Tiger" looked like a shrimp next to him. The dog was off-leash, and seemed to be by himself. There was nobody else in sight but me, Tiger, and this big furry beast.

Suddenly a woman came around the bend, saying what a cute puppy Tiger was. As she approached I could see she was holding a leash in her hand. Obviously, the big furry guy belonged to her. "Did you call my dog a puppy?" I said, feigning insult.

As she got closer I noticed that she was quite attractive. I teased that there was a whole lot of dog at the end of my leash. She smiled, hooking her dog back up. She introduced me and Tiger to him. His name was "Suki," and she called him "a monster but a lover." Her name was Jade, and she said she walked her dog in the park almost every day.

The four of us continued walking together. Jade said the park was convenient for them because she lived right around the corner. I said I was new to the neighborhood and Tiger and I were out exploring what it had to offer. Jade offered to give me some friendly neighborhood advice over a cup of fresh-brewed coffee and sweetened the invitation by promising home-baked muffins to go with it and doggy snacks for Tiger. How could I turn down such an appealing invitation?

A short distance from the park Jade stopped in front of a cute little house with a picket fence. She opened the front gate and both dogs rushed into the yard. I recognized the house and said I had often admired the landscaping when Tiger and I passed by. I needed some work done on my place, and strangely enough, I had almost knocked on the door to ask her who she used. Jade promised to give me her gardener's card, and we went inside for the grand tour before she put the coffee on. We left Suki and Tiger to entertain each other in the front yard.

Jade showed me around her cute little place, pointing out some of her favorite pieces. It was homey and decorated with a lot of taste. I noted that Suki had his own place of honor at the foot of her bed where he slept on a fluffy personalized pillow. Jade was obviously a full-fledged dog person; I was beginning to like her more and more.

She saved the master bath until last. It was her favorite place, she said, because she loved escaping from the world in a relaxing bath full of bubbles. I admit I was checking out more than the room at this point. I had admired Jade's breasts as we were walking the dogs, but hadn't noticed her curvy little figure until she stood in front of the full-length mirror across from the shower. She had a tight little ass and nice thighs that were emphasized by her short shorts.

She pointed out the Alpaca rug on the floor, which she had gotten on vacation in Peru. It was thick and fuzzy and she said she especially liked the way it felt against her skin when she got out of the shower and stepped on it. The image of her naked wet body stepping out of the steamy shower suddenly filled my mind. I had to really work at controlling myself because that was one sexy image!

I lost all control when she bent over to straighten out the rug. Her shorts rode up even higher on her butt. I got more than a little aroused at the sight of those tight round buns bent over in front of me. It's a good thing she was facing the other way, because my eyes were glued to her behind. I had to restrain myself from reaching out and caressing it.

As she straightened up and turned toward me, she lost her footing and stumbled. I caught her by her waist. She didn't pull away, but stood there, pressed against me. She gazed up at me; she had the prettiest eyes. I could feel her breasts against my chest, and her breathing had quickened. I was pretty sure about the signals I was getting from her, so I took a chance, acting on my impulse to cop a feel of her butt. I took a cheek in each hand and gave them a gentle little squeeze.

Jade didn't resist. In fact, she let me know it was okay by putting her hands around my neck and pulling me down to give me a juicy kiss. She was a great kisser. She had a seductive way with her tongue - sucking and teasing as she kissed. My nerve endings tingled as she rubbed her groin against mine. I felt our bodies heating up against each other. She put her hands on my butt and pulled me in closer.

Then she pulled away. I thought she had changed her mind about our potential amorous adventure. But she wasn't ending it... she had pulled back to untuck my shirt from my pants. She slid her hands up underneath it, caressing my chest. Her hands were warm and soft. Before I realized what I was doing, I pulled off her top. She responded with another kiss. I picked her up, sat her on the countertop and stood between her legs.

Unhooking her bra, I reached for her supple, perky breasts. She kissed the side of my face as I licked her nipples and worked my way up to her enticing lips. We kissed and nibbled on each other while I unzipped her shorts. She slid them off. She was wearing a tiny black thong underneath. Yum. I kissed her bellybutton.

Unzipping my pants, I stepped out of them. I continued to kiss and hug her. Jade reached into my boxers and massaged my dick. Oh man, I was so ready for her. I got hard right away. I lifted Jade off the counter and laid her on the soft fuzzy Alpaca rug. She was right... it felt silky and warm against my skin. I got down on my knees in front of her, and was looking straight at her luscious pussy.

I didn't want to rush into anything. I wanted to savor every sensation. I laid my dick on her stomach and slid it up and down, stopping every now and then to massage her clit. Jade smiled; she was getting into it. She reached down to stroke me. She really knew how to handle a man. I got thicker and harder with each sweet pull.

She raised her pelvis up to meet me, and I was ready. I rose up onto my knees, grabbed her ass and aimed my hard rod at her waiting pussy. I was so swollen I had to push myself in a little at a time. Jade was gently rocking her pelvis, guiding me deeper and deeper into her. Once I was all the way inside, she began to slide slowly back and forth on my dick.

She was one hot little momma, and her moves sent shivers rippling through me.

We were so attracted to each other that our bodies were about as close as they could get. Sparks were flying between us, and the smell of her hair and the softness of her skin titillated my senses. I stimulated her with my fingers while I was inside her and she loved it. Her body responded without hesitation to everything I did and she squealed to keep going… don't stop... keep doing it just like that.

I knew I was about to come, but Jade was in no mood to slow down. She gripped my butt and held on, pulling me further into her luscious body. I felt her contracting tighter and tighter, squeezing me inside until we were one. She tensed, and then released her sweet juices.

I couldn't hold back any longer. I came hard, right along with her. Jade arched her back, lifting both of us off the floor. She held on to me and screamed, and then she fell limp onto the rug, her eyes closed. I wrapped my arms around her and held her close.

When she opened her eyes, she kissed me and smiled. She said she'd never done anything like that in the bathroom before, and that it was out of this world. I agreed.

I told her I was sure glad I just happened to meet her at the park.

She smiled mischievously and wondered who would have thought that taking her dog for a walk would end up so deliciously? She suggested that next week, we try that little bar down the street.

I grinned and said, "Nah… we've already done that. How about the supermarket?"

Jade seemed to like that idea, musing that it could be fun to meet in the produce department... maybe by the melons.

I licked her nipple and said melons would be perfect... but we might also consider flirting over a big ripe cucumber. Jade laughed, holding my head in her hand, and said she loved our occasional roleplay games.

~~~

Someone else's house, the danger of being caught, and an unexpected lovemaking session in the middle of the day all add to John's excitement next...

John & Kelly
Sneaking it In

First and foremost, I want to state for the record that I love my in-laws. Everything is cool when they come to visit us. I love their company. But the one thing I do not like is when we have to visit them. They have a small house and there is absolutely no private space. Even if you talk softly, you can still be heard through the thin walls.

Those thin walls mean lovemaking drops to zilch, nada, nothing for me and my wife Kelly. I personally don't mind if someone hears me, but my wife can't bear the thought of her parents knowing she really enjoys sex. And let me tell you, my wife Kelly can get pretty wild when she's making love. When it's just me and her, it's no holds barred. But knowing her parents are in the next room, Kelly just does not want to go there.

Last month, Kelly and I had planned to go to our favorite lake for a week of relaxation. We had both been so busy and were looking forward to the getaway.

However, three weeks before our trip, Kelly's mom called and asked us to help with a celebration for Jodi, Kelly's younger sister. Jodi had just been awarded a fellowship to Harvard Law School, and it was certainly a significant award that called for celebration. But the timing was all wrong for us.

The vision of a week of romantic sunsets followed by wild and crazy sex had been my motivator to get through an unusually difficult project at work. Now I was struggling with the fact that our plans for this wonderful vacation time would have to wait. Instead we would be spending a week filled with little or perhaps NO sex at all!

True to my expectations, the moment we arrived at her mother's, Kelly was whisked away to help organize the catering. That left me to entertain myself. I went to the golf range to hit some balls. That's usually a great place for me to think about nothing but me, the golf club, and the ball. But the more I tried not to think about sex, the more I did think about it – of course – and the hornier I got. After hitting three buckets of balls trying to get it off my mind, I was bone tired and headed back to the house.

Everyone was home when I got there. The house was full of people, and some of them I'd never met before. Kelly greeted me with a warm hug and big smile. She said she'd be finished soon. I told her I was going to take a short nap and to be sure to wake me when she was done.

I must have fallen asleep immediately because I still had my cap on when Kelly plopped on top of me on the bed. Her warm body woke me from my lazy slumber, and I was still drowsy when she said she was going to take a bubble bath. She slapped my butt and climbed off the bed, moseying off toward the bathroom.

As I laid there listening to the sounds of the tub filling, I imagined making love to Kelly. There was nothing to take my mind off it now, and my body began to tingle. I was wide awake and I wanted to be with my wife. I jumped up, started undressing and headed for the bathroom. It looked like that was the only place I might get to be alone with my wife, so I took advantage of it. I hoped that in the privacy of the bathroom Kelly might not be so uptight about making love with me and wondering who could be listening.

Kelly had already slipped into a tub full of bubbles and was lying back with her eyes closed. I eased the door open and slipped into the shower. I let the warm water wash over me, rubbing it all over my body. When I stroked my hands over my rod, my body tensed with the anticipation of getting between Kelly's legs. I grabbed the bar of soap and lathered up. The feel of the warm water and the soapy lather combined with the vision of my naked wife in the bathtub was very erotic. I was definitely turning myself on and when I looked out at Kelly, she had joined in on the fun.

Her big brown areolas were like chocolate blossoms popping up through the bubbles. She was holding a breast in each hand, massaging the nipples with her fingertips. She circled the breast, and then squeezed the nipple. It must have felt good, because Kelly wore a devilish grin.

She had her head back and her eyes closed while she softly caressed her body, drifting away in her own fantasyland. As her hand traveled down, stroking between her legs, her cheeks flushed with color. She was pleasuring herself as only a woman can. I whispered that I wanted to join her. Her eyes slowly opened. She smiled at me but said no, she was busy right now, and I should go ahead and enjoy my shower.

Watching her, I was stroking my rod without even realizing how hard I was getting. I couldn't take my eyes off her. She looked delicious. I think she was deliberately teasing me. But how much can a man take? There was Kelly, lying serene and at peace with herself, while I, her horny husband, contemplated ravishing her beautiful body. I think she knew what effect she was having on me. I tried to be patient, soaking in the heat of the warm water and the invigorating massage of the pulsing showerhead.

I watched Kelly through the water cascading over my head. Her fingertips caressed her breasts. She was so gentle with herself and was enjoying it immensely. She slid down further into the water, raising her leg and rubbing it while she pointed her foot toward the ceiling. Her movements were slow and sensuous. It was as if this was the first time she had touched herself. She gently ran her hands over her curves, appreciating her own body. She began to move like she was making love and responding to her lover's touch. Her fingers moved down to between her legs.

At first her strokes appeared to be very soft. She stopped to linger and play in the curly hairs of her bush. Then she pushed her fingers deeper into the folds of her pussy. Her fingers were probing for her pleasure zone. She slid them up and down and began to squirm. As she continued to stroke herself, she opened her legs wider. She was applying more pressure on her clit and it was becoming increasingly difficult for her to lay still.

Although we were apart, this watery, erotic playtime was blowing my mind. It was as if we were making love to each other from afar. The more she massaged her clit, the harder I stroked myself. My body was tense with sexual energy and I was imagining how ready Kelly's body would be to receive me.

I lost track of time. I had lathered and rubbed my body until everything felt tight. My rod was standing straight out

71

and was immensely swollen. With the water still pouring over my head, I gave Kelly "that look." Her eyes were open now and she smiled, knowing what I wanted without me uttering a word. She licked her lips and in a sexy sweet voice said she was ready for me now.

In a flash, I shut off the water and was out of the shower. I bent to kiss Kelly as I stepped into the tub behind her. I knew I was going to have to pace myself, but I wanted to get into her so badly. We kissed hungrily and I savored the sweetness of her lips. She pushed her backside into my groin. Her golden tanned body glistened as the water dripped from her slender shoulders. I planted soft kisses all over her back and made my way down, tenderly kissing the cheeks of her butt.

I was so turned on. I continued to kiss along the crease, making my way to her pleasure zone. I like touching Kelly and discovering every secret erogenous zone on her body. And she knows it. She leaned forward on her knees and opened her legs to give me better access to her bush; I could tell she was ready. Her lips had swollen and I had to spread them with my tongue. The taste was so sweet I couldn't stop licking.

Then Kelly sat up and turned around, kissing me. She gently lifted my throbbing rod and bent over to suck it as she stroked my abs. It was hard to contain myself. Kelly began to playfully tap my rod against her lips as she continued to lick me.

I was really close to climaxing, when, with perfect timing, she stopped. She sat up and presented her beautiful breasts to me. What a pleasure! My lips eagerly accepted the gift and my tongue relished the tenderness of her skin. I proceeded to give her breasts a tongue massage, one after the other. Then I licked her cute little bellybutton. We were both ready for more. Kelly straddled my body and let me enter her.

She began to move up and down on me, and watching her beautiful body merge with mine was making me sizzle. Our bodies joined in an erotic water dance, so tender, so joyful and so exhilarating. Each time our bodies pumped, our hearts pounded and our senses heightened. Kelly knew that I was close to climaxing again and slid off me.

We stood up and kissed tenderly while I caressed up and down her body. She turned and offered her backside. I slipped my rod into her and her swollen lips surrounded it, gripping me firmly. Kelly raised her leg and set it on the edge of the tub so I could massage her clit. The suction between our bodies was so tight and slippery and the sensations on her clit so intense that Kelly became very vocal.

She can get real noisy when she's enjoying herself, and she was moaning so loudly I had to shush her. She had forgotten where we were. She laughed softly and thanked me for reminding her.

I suggested we try sitting on the edge of the tub. I placed a towel over the rim and sat down, one leg in the tub and the other out so I could balance myself. I leaned back and Kelly slid onto my rod, riding me like a bucking bronco. The more I stroked her clit, the wilder her thrusting became. We were locked in rhythm in a world of our own, forgetting all about the thin walls. We were talking nasty to each other and egging each other on, driven by pure animal magnetism. I wanted nothing but to be here with her and she felt the same.

Our bodies continued to slam together. Then we were there. The moment of release came crashing upon us. Kelly was moaning and sighing loudly, as usual, but I was trying to keep quiet. When I came, it was so intense I began to tell Kelly everything I was feeling. I couldn't keep quiet anymore.

I squeezed her tighter and tapped my fingers on her clit. Then she came, too, her body uncontrollably sliding back and forth on my rod. I felt her contractions gripping me. We were lost in time... the only thing we could do was wait for the contractions to stop so our bodies could relax.

I think we both realized at the same time that being quiet was something we'd forgotten all about. Kelly laughed when she heard voices as someone passed by outside the bathroom. We hugged, kissed and leaned back to savor our rare moment of solitude at her parents' house.

I had been worried that this was going to be a week without sex. But here we were, locked in embrace after one of the most mind-blowing lovemaking sessions we had ever had.

The unexpected pleasures are sometimes the best ones!

~~~

For men, there's one fantasy that's more common than any other... the threesome.

"Yeah, I've fantasized about having a three-way with my wife quite a few times. I mean, the thought of having another woman in bed with us is just awesome. I don't know about another guy but the thought of another woman does something to me."

"Having sex with two women would be great. I've fantasized about it. I've never actually done it, though it's certainly on my list of things I'd like to try."

"I'll tell you, after some experiences, I believe one woman's more than enough for me. They're very complex!"

"One of my favorite fantasies would be a three-way with my wife. As a matter of fact, I had a dream about it last week."

Scott indulged his threesome fantasy only in his mind, while enjoying actual physical pleasure with his partner.

Scott & Emily
A Bed for Three

I have a beautiful girlfriend and I totally enjoy making love to her. She's the only woman in the world for me. I don't need anybody but her. But I admit, every now and then I fantasize about a threesome. I picture my beautiful girlfriend Emily and me in bed, joined by another woman, and Emily enjoying it just as much as me. That must have been on my mind as I fell off to sleep the other night. The last thing I remember is curling up against Emily and whispering, "Sweet dreams."

Then next thing I knew, I was woken by voices. Someone was asking whether "it was alright." I didn't recognize the voice. I was in bed by myself and my first thought was wondering where Emily was, so I got up and followed the sound of the voices. They were coming from the guest bedroom. When I got to the doorway, I saw Emily and a beautiful blonde woman in the shower. The two women were embracing and caressing each other.

They saw me standing in the doorway and beckoned

for me to join them. I didn't hesitate. I stepped into the shower and the women opened their arms to include me in their embrace.

And then, I woke up. I was still in bed beside Emily. She had turned over in her sleep, waking me from that lovely dream. I pulled her closer and revived the image in my mind. Before I knew it, I had dozed off again.

Lucky for me I went back to Dreamland. I was still bed, with Emily snuggled up close behind me. But in the dream, we weren't alone. The beautiful, sandy-haired blonde was in front of me, sleeping with her butt pressing into my groin. From behind, Emily was pressing her breasts into my back. Her thigh rested on my leg. I rose up and looked at the two of them sleeping peacefully.

The women stirred. The blonde opened her eyes and smiled. Then Emily opened her eyes and reached out to rub my arm. It was like she was saying it was okay. So I laid down on the bed between them, stretched out on my back. The two women rose up, kneeling in front of me. They were both so beautiful. They didn't say anything and neither did I. I just stared, and they smiled at me with mischief in their eyes. I felt like a kid in a candy store, grinning from cheek to cheek.

The ladies sat back, one on each side of my body. Emily leaned over, kissing my thighs, working her way up to my navel. The other woman caressed my chest and pinched my nipples. I slipped into a state of euphoria, my body tingling from their touch.

I reached up to Emily, but she took my arm and laid it back at my side. I wasn't expected to do anything... just lay back and enjoy. No problem! I closed my eyes, delighting in the warm fingers moving down to my groin. I knew there were four hands on me, but the sensation felt like there were forty.

Suddenly I was enveloped in warmth and moisture. My mind filled with erotic images. Opening my eyes, I saw both women licking my cock. What an amazing sight! They started at the base of my shaft and slowly ran their silky tongues up to the tip. It was incredible watching them take turns slipping me through their juicy lips. It felt like I was sliding into velvet.

The way they took turns was a unique sensation because they each had a different technique. I tried to hold myself back; this was too good to be true. I wanted it to last as long as possible, but watching them pleasure me with their mouths was putting me over the edge.

Emily could sense it. She moved off my cock and stood up over my head, slowly lowering her pussy toward my face. She smiled and said it was time to eat. I didn't need to be told twice. I put my hungry lips up against her. She rested on one knee as she rolled over my tongue. I grabbed her butt and pulled her closer so I could get deeper. Emily was getting very excited; I could tell by the way she moved her body across my face. The sensation of going down on Emily while the blonde woman sucked on me was almost more than I could stand.

The blonde took a break, lying back and watching us. She was so sexy... making no effort to hide the fact that observing Emily and me was turning her on. I wanted to get her back in on the action. I rose up and flipped Emily onto her stomach, landing her on top of the other woman.

They started kissing each other very gently. Gazing into each other's eyes, they smiled as if they'd known each other for a long time. Emily nuzzled the blonde's neck and the blonde responded by holding Emily's face in her hands and kissing her deeply. Watching the way they touched each other turned me rock hard again. Emily was on top and her perky butt looked irresistible. I caressed her soft cheeks and she reached out and took my arm, pulling me toward her. I knew what she wanted, so I slid between her cheeks and gently entered her. I could tell she liked it by her moan. She was still kissing the blonde. Watching them, I thrust deeper and deeper into her pussy. The blonde looked up at me from underneath as Emily moaned louder. I knew I was going to come any minute.

Suddenly Emily reached back and pulled me out. She rolled off the blonde and onto her back. The blonde responded immediately, getting on her knees and going down on Emily. Her butt was wagging back and forth in front of me. I couldn't resist the opportunity, so I slid into the blonde's pussy. The room filled with sexual tension and sensual sounds. We were all close to climaxing.

The girls didn't want it to end yet. They slowed down to catch their breath and switched positions. The blonde lay back with her legs spread wide open. Emily moved between them, her tongue lingering on the blonde's clit. She licked up and down and side to side, and then nibbled on it. The blonde woman moaned, pinching her own nipples and gyrating her pelvis in response to Emily's touch. I had never seen – or really ever even thought about – Emily with another woman. I knew it would drive me crazy jealous if she was with another man, but watching her enjoy the blonde's body was a whole different trip.

I was trembling with sexual tension. I had to get between somebody's legs fast. Emily's butt was pointed at me and I jumped on it, clamping my thighs around her cheeks and slipping into her. She shuttered as I entered, the three of us immersed in the connection with each other. Emily kept licking the blonde's pussy, and now she was also pumping her finger in and out of her. At the same time, Emily was moaning and groaning every time I thrust into her. I was in a frenzy, pushing deeper and deeper as she pumped her finger deeper into the blonde in response. The air was filled with the anticipation of sexual release.

The blonde couldn't hold out one minute longer. While Emily continued to pleasure her pussy, the blonde came hard. Her body rose up off the bed and she screamed. She collapsed back down onto the bed and Emily rested her head on her abdomen. The blonde continued to stroke Emily's hair and watch me make love to her.

I slid out and rubbed my tip over Emily's flower. I massaged it and rubbed it until she started to shiver and I knew it was time. Then I gently entered her again and pumped slowly. Emily's body responded with a shudder, and she pulled me into her. I knew she wanted me to give her all I had. I did just that. I drove into her, hard and deep. Her muscles contracted and our bodies fused together. The connection was exquisite. I felt her come, and I responded with an explosion. We climaxed harder than we ever had before.

I fell on top of Emily and we all lay quietly, gently stroking one another. Emily smiled and sighed, asking me how I felt. I told her she was incredible. The blonde smiled and sighed, saying she felt great and that she had never done anything like this before.

As we lay there, my mind flashed back to what had just happened. I smiled, tingling again at the thought of both women pleasuring my cock. I relived it in all its glorious detail… Emily and the blonde taking turns sliding up and down on me, licking and sucking my cock like their favorite lollipop. I remembered the different techniques they each used, one just as pleasurable as the other.

I reveled in the memory of going down on my girlfriend while the blonde sucked my cock.

The feeling was incredible and I held the image in my mind, savoring it. I remembered the feel of the blonde's pussy when I pounded it while she was licking Emily. The images were just as exciting as the feelings and I realized I was getting aroused again. I pictured my girlfriend's perky butt wagging at me and how unbelievable it felt when I slipped my hard cock in between those firm round cheeks.

My thoughts were on fire with the vision of watching the two beautiful women take turns kissing and going down on each other... Emily doing her thing on the blonde's pussy, pumping her finger in and out of her while she licked and sucked her clit... and it made me hornier than ever. What a turn-on this night had been!

And then suddenly, it all dissolved. I awoke with a start. I was lying in my bed, with Emily lying next to me as usual, sound asleep. I sat up and looked around for the blonde woman. Where was she? Where did she go? I took a couple of deep breaths to clear my head, and realized that she had only existed in my sweet sexy dream.

A fleeting thought of all the love and sex I had savored that night passed through my now wide-awake mind. It felt as good as any real life memory I had. I licked my lips, re-membering the sweet taste of the two sexy women in my dream. Emily was still asleep. I kissed her on the cheek. "Sweet dreams, darling," I whispered, wondering if her imagination was taking her anywhere near as erotic as where I had just been.

~~~

Sexual Secrets and Erotic Encounters

Real couples. Real sex. Real life.

Part 2

What Women Want

Here's what some of the women we spoke to said:

"Women want to be desired. They want to feel wanted; they want to feel like their body is accepted. They don't want to feel like they have to be perfect or have the perfect breasts or the perfect body. They want to be loved for their insides as well as their outsides."

"I want someone that's very gentle and kind and loving."

"I'd say men need to know that women need more attention than men usually give."

"I like it if he really focuses his attention on me."

"I love being romanced, loved and adored."

The first story comes from Beverley, who had a special evening with her husband Ted when he planned a simple but quite romantic surprise for her...

82

Beverley & Ted
Sweet and Juicy

Ted always knows how to make me feel loved and adored. One night last week when I got home, I was so tired I even had trouble opening the door. I could never have guessed what Ted had planned for me. As I stepped inside, he was standing right there in front of me, a big grin on his face and his eyes sparkling. He kissed me and scooped me up in his arms, nuzzling my nose and neck.

I like homecomings like that! Just thinking about it gets me tingly.

Ted carried me effortlessly into the bedroom, telling me to watch my head as he dipped and turned to get us through the doorway. With a tender look on his face he said, "Beverley, tonight's gonna be your night, honey." He gently laid me in the center of the bed and placed a small, soft pillow under my neck. He kneeled by my feet. I was filled with anticipation and forgot all about being tired. "So it's gonna be my night, huh?" I smiled. Ted moved closer, gently rubbing my legs and feet.

"I've got some special treats for you," he said. "Like what?" I asked, with no idea what he had in mind. "Well... I know how much you like apples and bananas," he said playfully. "So we'll start with this." He reached over to the nightstand and picked up a luscious tray of fruit, placing it on the bed next to me. That was definitely not something I expected!

"Look at all this!" I squealed with delight. Ted leaned forward and said, "I'm gonna treat you like a queen tonight." He plucked a cluster of grapes and dangled them over my head. "I think this is how they feed royalty," he teased, lowering a luscious grape into my mouth. I did feel like a queen!

Sucking the grape into my mouth I savored the sweet juiciness. Tilting my head back, I closed my eyes, opened my mouth and waited for another one. Ted moved closer and this time fed me a grape from his lips, squirting the juice into my mouth, then licking the juice droplets off my lips. Our tongues met and slowly explored each other. "Oh, Beverley, you do that so well," Ted said.

"Next up, tangerines," he whispered, putting a slice between his teeth and presenting it to my mouth. The tart citrus was a perfect companion to his sweet and tender kiss. I loved being treated like pampered royalty!

I seductively nibbled on the tangerine, eyes closed, circling it with my tongue to tease him. I think Ted was enjoying it even more than I was! "You know, we don't do this enough," he said. "And I don't say I love you enough. But I do... I love you very much." That melted me. I pulled him close. We hugged and kissed. His touch was tender and his kiss was delicious. I could have stayed like that all night... but Ted wasn't done yet.

84

"And now, one of your favorites," he said, as he placed a strawberry slice in his mouth. Leaning forward, he caressed my shoulders, and slipped my bra straps down. My breasts fell out, nipples standing at attention. Ted's eyes twinkled as he bent and circled my nipples with the strawberry slice. I was tingling with sensation. He flicked my nipples with the berry, and then delivered it to my waiting lips. I sucked it in, along with his eager tongue.

Ted retreated for a moment, teasing me. His eyes focused on my breasts. Reaching out, he gently cupped them, giving them a firm squeeze. Then he sucked in one of my nipples. That sucking sensation drives me wild! The feeling was even more intense when I closed my eyes. Ted was into the moment, so I laid back and let him go. I wondered if he was having the same fantasy I was of a queen floating away down the Nile.

He took his time, each breast a delightful feast to be savored. I can still picture him with his eyes closed, moving from one to the other and back again.

When he opened his eyes again and let go of my nipple, he picked up an apple slice. He said he didn't expect me to eat the whole thing and I couldn't help laughing as he put the wedge in his mouth. It looked like a big red smile!

I can't remember the last time he was so playful and sexy. He poked that apple wedge in and out of my mouth very suggestively. I grabbed him by the back of the neck, pulled him to me and bit it, pulling it out of his mouth. I tongued it, slowly pushing it in and out as Ted watched, captivated. I made love to that slice of apple, sucking it, licking it, nibbling it, and then seductively licked off my fingers. I put on quite a show for him. As I savored the last morsel, Ted reached for the platter again.

"Oh, yeah," he said, laughing and picking up a banana, "Now

for the most dangerous of all." He waved it in front of me and I snatched it from him, rubbing the tip around my nipples. I don't know what came over me, but I became a sultry, hot mama. I teased Ted, telling him I was thinking about his big hard dick as I sucked the banana in and out of my mouth, playfully holding and stroking it like it was him. I rubbed it against my nipples, coating them with the sweet, sticky flavor of the tropics.

Ted was totally worked up now. He slid my panties off and ran his fingertips over the little patch of hair covering my mound. The warmth of his hands, the smell of the banana, and the cool air on my nipples were intoxicating. "Ah, Beverley, you have such a beautiful body!" he said admiringly. I wanted him to make love to me right then, and he knew it!

One flick of his arms and he shed his robe. We were both naked. He gently rubbed his chest up and down my body from my abdomen to my breasts. I was tingling. He took his time and it made me even more excited. I pulled him toward me, intent on giving him pleasure as well.

This was one of the most sensual experiences we'd had together. Ted was loving me with his eyes and his hands and every part of his body. "Now," he leaned forward and said, "I'm going to clean off these nipples." He slowly licked from the bottom of my breast up to the nipple, and sucked it into his mouth. He pulled on it, stretching it gently as he sucked. I could tell he liked it as much as I did, because I felt him getting harder against me. I pulled him in closer. He caressed my breasts like precious gems, his movements deliberate, firm, slow and titillating.

"Now, for a little added flavor," he said, reaching toward the nightstand and picking up a glass of wine. He dipped his finger in and rubbed it around my nipples. "A fine wine for a fine lady," he whispered. I tilted my head back and closed my eyes, soaking up the tingling feeling from his fingertip caresses. I felt so loved. "You're such a sweetheart," I whispered.

He took another sip of wine and kissed me, the sweet oaky flavor of the wine permeating his lips. We were both throbbing with passion now and I was craving more. I lifted my legs to caress his back. He said that taking his time making love was making it so much more fun. I nodded...this was truly wonderful. Ted reveled in the smell and taste of my body. He slowly slid his tongue down my chest to my belly button, moving lower and planting little kisses. I quivered as he buried his face in me.

We were in another world. As he slowly nuzzled the patch of hair above my clit, he paused and slid his tongue toward my right thigh, then - Oh! He found the key to unlock me! My thighs opened wider and I gave him full access. I know it was a divine sight for him. He slowly but firmly stuck his tongue on my clit and I raised my legs to surround his neck. I held on and pulled him in as he licked and sucked me. I closed my eyes and pleasure washed over me. My body was rocking. I pushed my body into his, wanting more.

It got so good. I raised my pelvis, opened my legs even wider, and braced them on Ted's shoulders as I thrust upward. The pleasure I got from his warm, sensuous tongue was unbearable.

My body exploded. I had one of the best orgasms I've ever had with my husband. It was so good. I held on tight, moaning with pleasure.

With a long sigh, I fell back on the bed. Ted never missed a lick. He rolled with my body and continued pleasuring me with his tongue, working his way back up my body.

He kissed my thighs, and then ran his slick tongue up past my belly button and stomach to my still erect nipples. I raised my head to meet his hungry tongue. We kissed deeply.

I felt like he was touching the inner core of my soul. The air was charged with passion. Ted gently laid over me, holding me tightly. "I love you," I said joyfully. He kissed me and said, "Beverley, I love *you!*"

Every time I think about that night, my body heats up. I felt so beautiful and loved. Ted made me feel so special. It took time and thought for him to put together that evening, and it was well worth it! My body and soul opened up to receive him because I felt so loved… so adored.

I'll never forget that night!

~~~

"Men need to give as much as they take."

"I like him to be romantic. A type of guy who won't be afraid to cry in front of you."

"The biggest turn on to me is to see my husband playing with my children on the floor or just interacting with them."

"The biggest thing men should know about women is that when a woman is telling you something, and telling you their feelings, all they want you to do is listen."

"Come in the kitchen, help me cook. If you don't know how to peel carrots, I'll show you how to peel carrots."

"I like it when a man cooks for me. It makes me feel like

he's trying to please me... that it's important to him to please me... he wants to make me happy. And fixing food for someone is such a nurturing act."

When Brian surprises his wife Joanne with a lovingly prepared meal, his thoughtfulness turns up the heat...

Joanne & Brian

Food for Love

One night, when I got home from work, I walked into the kitchen and saw that my husband Brian was cooking. Now, that might not seem like much, but Brian never cooks. Brian doesn't even know how to cook. But there he was with pots going on every burner! He was even dressed for the occasion in a blue chef's apron. He was having a great time, smiling and singing. I asked him what was up, and he said, "I'm cooking dinner for my lady." I looked around and teasingly asked, "What lady?" "My one and only," he answered, "You."

"Are you OK?" I asked, "Did something happen? You never cook!" "Well, I do now," he said, "and you're going to have the best dinner ever." Grinning from ear to ear, he steered me out of the kitchen and said, "Go get comfortable, Joanne. Have a seat. Dinner will be ready in five minutes."

I was tired from standing on my feet all day but just then it didn't matter. My man was in the kitchen cooking for me and making me feel very special. I sat at the dining room table and quickly began to relax. Brian had turned down the lights and lit some candles, throwing a warm glow throughout the room. I leaned back in my chair listening to the soft music he had playing, taking it all in. Everything was wonderful.

Then Brian walked in with two dinner plates. He was so proud of his creations. I have to admit that the dish was somewhat unrecognizable. But he was so pleased with it, I wasn't about to burst his bubble. "Wow, it looks great," I said. "What do you call it?"

He said he just called it what it was: a little chicken, a little spinach, some carrots, some croutons, and some lasagna. He was so sweet. I told him it looked delicious. And the aroma was making me really hungry. The look on his face said he needed the reassurance. No matter how it tasted, I was going to enjoy it... he had worked hard to do all this just for me.

He gestured for me to start eating and disappeared for a moment, coming back with a bottle of red wine. He poured some and asked me to taste it. I was impressed.... It was a good choice to go with his dinner. He was full of surprises tonight, because he never showed much interest in choosing wine before... that had always been my domain. He said it had taken him a while to pick it out and he was glad I liked it.

I could tell he was worn out from cooking... he wasn't used to how much effort it can take! I wanted to do something nice for him in return, so I moved over to his lap and hand-fed him some chicken. He laughed while he nibbled on it. I kissed him and then fed him a mouthful of veggies. When he was done chewing, I kissed him again. This whole "making-dinner-for-the-wife" thing was surprisingly arousing. One kiss led to another and then there we were, making out big time at the dining room table!

I stood up and swung my leg over his lap, straddling him. Holding his face in my hands and kissing him deeply, I felt him get hard. He wrapped his arms around me and slid them up under my blouse, stroking my back. I unbuttoned his shirt and caressed his chest, playfully licking his nipples. He unbuttoned my blouse and slid my breast out of my bra, lovingly cupping it and sucking my nipple until it was hard and erect. He unhooked my bra, sliding it off, and I was naked from the waist up, rubbing my breasts against his bare chest.

Brian eased me off his lap and unbuckled his belt. While he took his pants off, I slithered out of my skirt. "Leave your high heels on," he whispered. That made me smile. He sat down and I straddled him again, naked except for my fabulous high heels. It made me feel quite sexy.

The food and the effort Brian had put into cooking were the best foreplay. I was completely aroused before he even touched my pussy. And Brian was hard as a rock. He gently slid into my moist body. It felt incredible. I clamped on tighter as he leaned me back and sucked on my nipples. I was intensely aroused now, chills running up my spine. He moved his hands down around my waist and thrust me up and down onto him. I leaned back, gasping for air. The pleasure was almost unbearable.

I felt so uninhibited and so loved. My body was responding to his thoughtfulness as much as to his touch. He gently eased out of me and we stood up. He turned me around and pulled my backside into him, wrapping his arms around me. As he slid into me again, I was smiling from ear to ear. This night was getting better and better. I massaged my clit while Brian thrust in and out of me, over and over.

I slowed him down because I knew I was about to come and I didn't want it to end yet. I was enjoying this so much! Our bodies were fused together like we were one.

Brian was squeezing my butt and I could tell he was on the verge of bursting. He kept saying "Oh yeah, Joanne, oh yeah..." He was in another world. We were both lost in the passion. The more I massaged my clit the more of him I wanted. I savored every tingle.

He was totally absorbed in the moment, rhythmically sliding in and out of me. A surge of energy shot through me, and I told him I was there! "I'm gonna come, baby!" I whispered, and he let himself go. We both peaked, my orgasm erupting through my entire body in a sizzling heat wave. I tensed tight as a drum, and then released, exhausted.

Flopping back onto the dining room table, I knocked over Brian's dinner plate. He fell on top of me, equally spent. We lay there silently, catching our breath.

When we finally looked at each other, we burst out laughing. Wow. The combination of sexual release and laughter felt great!

I must say, even though Brian isn't a very good cook, that meal will always be one of my favorites. It was far more satisfying than expected. Maybe it's because by the time we were done making love, I was hungry enough to eat anything!

~~~

"I want someone you can trust and do lots of stuff with...nice things and sexy things."

"I like confidence. And I'm looking for stability... long term... and no games."

"Just don't lie, you know? If you have something to say just let it out in the open, because then women are gonna be more understanding and they're gonna like the fact that you're

telling the truth rather than holding it from them."

"I want someone who doesn't lie to me. Deception will absolutely make me crazy."

"I guess honesty is a good one, because you really need to be open and discuss what things make you happy and what makes him happy. And the more open you are, really, the better it is."

Carol Anne found out it was okay to show her boyfriend how she pleasures herself when she was literally "caught in the act"… and it turned into an evening that strengthened their relationship…

Carol Anne & Lance
The Pleasure's All Mine

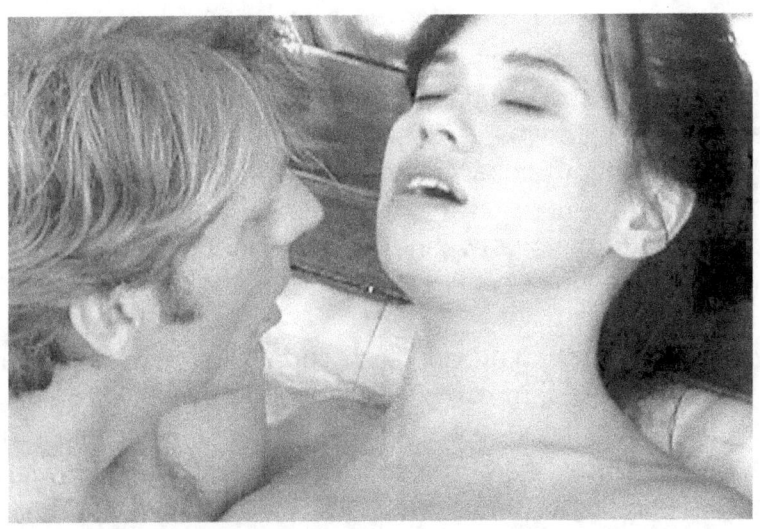

For me, one of the most important parts of my sexuality is when I have time to myself. I like to explore my body. It's something I've come to learn about myself.

When I first started making love, it was all about the guy pleasing me. If he was experienced I usually had a good time. But I've been with a few guys who didn't really care what turned me on, and unfortunately, those experiences were kinda funky.

As I've grown more interested in finding out what *I* like, I've gotten more relaxed about spending time discovering new things about my own body. I've gotten really good at bringing myself to an orgasm now... but up until last week, I never told my boyfriend Lance that. I assumed that of course he knew, but it wasn't something we ever talked about. It was something I would do when he wasn't home. Until last week.

I got home a little early and the house was empty. Lance wasn't due to be home from work for an hour or two.

So I slipped into my silk negligee and got comfortable in bed with a trashy romance novel - a fun escape from a hard day's work.

As usual, I got myself worked up pretty quickly. Reading steamy scenes of a hunky guy taking you is titillating, and before I knew it I was caressing my breasts and my nipples. My fingers unconsciously moved to the soft skin of my tummy and across the tops of my thighs. By the next page I was caressing the hairs between my legs. Heat rose up, spreading over my abdomen.

I was feeling flushed outside and slippery inside when I heard Lance clear his throat. "Carol Anne?" he softly asked. I snapped out of it and looked up, and there he was, poking his head around the bedroom door. "Hey there," he said, with a devilish grin on his face.

I was momentarily speechless. Lance came in and sat on the bed next to me. He didn't say anything else, just kissed me. For some reason, for the first time, I felt like talking about what I was doing. "Honey," I said, "You do know that I masturbate, right?" He said of course he knew... he masturbated, and he would have been surprised if I didn't.

I appreciated hearing him say that. I think we had both made assumptions about the other, but now that the subject was out in the open, we could share our private experiences. It could only make things better between us. I wanted to actually show Lance how I masturbated, but I got shy again. He looked at me so affectionately, softly stroking my arm. I really wanted to go there with him... I wanted him to see what really turns me on... but it wasn't easy. I pulled him closer and held him for a moment, my eyes closed, gathering my courage.

Then I reached for my lube and put little dab on the tip of my middle finger. Moving my finger inside the folds of my pussy,

I rubbed it lightly over my clit. My juices started flowing and my vagina relaxed. I use gentle circular movements all around my clit, working the lube in with the flat part of my fingers.

Just like always, I got aroused pretty fast. I told Lance how good it felt. I took his hand and placed it on top of my clit while I continued to massage, it so he could feel exactly what I was doing. I kept my hand on top of his and guided him through my pleasure spots. I helped him feel the amount of pressure I like and how slippery I wanted it. Lance said he could feel changes in my body as I massaged. He felt my temperature rise and the moisture increase on the surface of my skin and in my pussy. The look on his face told me he was enjoying this as much as I was.

Together, Lance and I continued exploring my body. I can feel his hands on me right now as I think about how good it was. I remember grabbing his hand and saying, "Do this here... work it in like that... right there feels really good." The more we explored my body together, the more I wanted to show him. I wasn't embarrassed anymore, because he was so into it. He was listening and watching and asking what felt best.

I told him my clit needs lots of attention. I showed him how to put his fingers down between the lips, stroke the clit, and then slip his finger into my vagina, thrusting it in and out. Then back to the clit, then thrusting in and out again. That really turns up the heat for me. Each time I showed him something that felt good, he wanted to try doing it to me.

Lance was such a good student. He watched my every move. It was the greatest form of communication I'd ever experienced between us. We were talking with our hands, mouths and eyes. Sharing and practicing was a lot of fun. I got comfortable with my demonstration, and frankly, a little greedy. After all the demonstrating, I wanted to just lay back and have him do me.

He had it down! It was an exhilarating experience. I continued coaching... "Oh yeah, just like that... now a little more pressure with that one finger." Lance made it easy for me to tell him exactly what I wanted. He listened and then tried my suggestions, his skills improving on the spot.

I leaned back and let my body relish the experience. It was getting better by the minute. Lance was touching my body exactly the way I like it and my body was responding. I made sure to let him know every time he did something especially pleasurable.

It was as if we were legendary lovers. I felt so close to him. It was an important milestone, realizing I could be myself with Lance and not be embarrassed about showing him exactly what I liked. It was really hot - like I was making passionate love to him, even though I was just lying back and receiving pleasure. I told him it was better than anything he'd ever done to me before.

His fingertips took me slowly up and then he'd change the speed. My heart quickened and my body tingled with anticipation of an incredible orgasm.

I grabbed his face and kissed him deeply, slipping my tongue into his mouth. I felt an irresistible urge to have him go down on me, so I came right out and asked him if he could lick me while he was fingering me.

He didn't say a word... he just crawled over between my legs and pushed them wide open. I watched his head go down and felt his soft, wet tongue lick me as his finger circled on my clit. I closed my eyes and drifted into my pleasure zone. My body was responding to his touch in a way I'd never experienced with him before. My pelvis thrust up and down. I wanted to feel his tongue hit my G-spot, so I urged him on to it.

I swear my man has a magic touch; the more he stroked me, the more I wanted. His caresses felt incredible. And then I was there... the moment when I feel like I just can't take any more.

My body throbbed - tensing and releasing as Lance massaged and pressured my clit. Oh yeah, it was way beyond good having my man lick and finger me exactly the way I like it. My mind and body were in perfect sync with his fingers and tongue. I was so wet. He kept licking and sucking, thrusting his finger in and out of me, and I just kept coming. It was amazing.

Even remembering it can make me wet again. If I had known how much it would increase the pleasure I received by talking about it and showing Lance how I like to do myself, I would have been talking and showing long ago! I hate that I wasted so much time being shy. And I'm thankful I got over it. So much sweet love came from knowing I could trust my man enough to share my secrets with him.

~~~

"Physically, in a man, I like their upper body. I'm turned on by their chest and their arms."

"Their chest and their arms, for sure. And their rear end!"

"A good smile. And healthy... fit."

"A great smile and eyes."

"I'm in a relationship. I look for open-mindedness and respect toward women."

"I like eyes, smile, a sense of humor and self-confidence."

"Obviously, I'm gonna check out the looks first. Although I know that won't last, so what I'll look for after that is what's inside - the personality."

"If they're confident, is real appealing to me."

In the next story, more than any specific physical attribute, it was her husband's self-confidence and sense of humor that convinced Dee she could spring an adventurous surprise on him – and know he'd most likely go along with it...

Dee & Larry

Welcome Arrival

Whenever my husband Larry goes on a business trip, I really miss him. My life seems to move in slow motion when he's not with me. I have two young children and they can fill every minute of my time, so you know I'm really horny and longing for him if my life moves slowly!

The last time he left town on business, I planned a very special homecoming. I like to reminisce about it, and it always makes me grin.

To begin with, Larry has a big, beautiful smile. It's the first thing you notice about him, along with his sparkling caramel-brown eyes. Those are the two things that first attracted me. And after five years of marriage, one way he still keeps me interested is the great sense of humor behind those sparkling eyes. He's not afraid to laugh at himself or find humor in whatever is happening… maybe because he's got just the right amount of self-confidence. His confidence is what really turns me on.

After his last business trip, I really missed him - as usual - and decided to surprise him when I picked him up at the airport. I called my mother and arranged for her to take care of the kids for a few hours. I wasn't sure yet exactly what my surprise for Larry would be, but I knew I wanted us to be alone. I thought about taking him straight to dinner, or maybe even dancing, because we haven't done that for a while. And then it struck me how to make it really different - I'd do something he would never expect me to do in public.

I started preparing the night before he came home. After the children were in bed, I filled the tub with bath oil in Larry's favorite fragrance. I soaked myself, read a book and enjoyed a glass of wine. I have one of those book trays that hooks across the tub, leaving your hands free, so I could read and rub the bubbles over my body at the same time. Their silky feel on my skin was turning me on. I thought about how much I missed Larry and looked forward to his return.

Larry always says he loves my soft skin. So I buffed and polished myself from head to toe. When I got out of the tub, I finished my spa treatment by applying body oil in the same fragrance. Then I finalized my plan for the next day. I felt like mixing something old with something new. The new was going to be how I greeted him, and the old would be a favorite place where we used to go. I went to bed excited, wondering how he would react.

My Mom was on time the next day and the children were happy to see her. I was glad to have them off my mind and well-tended-to for a while. We said goodbye and I headed to the airport. As I approached the terminal, there he was, standing at the curb by the baggage claim, waiting for me like always.

When he saw me drive up, his big smile flashed and he moved quickly toward the car. I jumped out and gave him a big hug and kiss. "How was your trip?" I asked. He said he was tired, but all had gone well. He had closed a big deal, so his satisfaction tempered his tiredness. He gave me another hug and told me he missed me. He opened the car door for me, like the gentleman he always is, and I got into the passenger side.

When he climbed in behind the wheel, I grinned and told him we had to celebrate his new deal. He was all for that and gave me another luscious kiss. I told him I missed him so much. He pulled me close, kissed me again and whispered, "Not like I missed you and the kids. Where are they anyway?" At home, I told him, with my mom, and having a great time.

We got going, and as Larry slowed down for the first stop sign, I told him I had a surprise for him. He was so focused on driving that he hadn't noticed I was unbuckling the belt on my coatdress. There was a red light ahead, and when we stopped for it, I flashed Larry... revealing that I was wearing my white thigh-high nylons, satin lace garter belt, and no panties or bra.

I have full round breasts, and they bounced out of the coat, the pale brown nipples standing at attention. I asked him if he liked what he saw, and he answered by licking his lips and nodding his head. He was pretty much speechless! After staring for a moment, he asked if this meant we were going to "the point". I smiled coyly and nodded, closing up my coat.

Larry let out a hearty laugh. There was a beep behind us... the signal had turned green. But Larry didn't want to go without another kiss. I gave him a quick peck to avoid another beep, and we headed off for "the point". I could tell he was anxious to get there... he was driving a little faster than usual.

Watching him, I felt such a rush of desire. He was my partner for life. I told him I didn't know what I would do if I ever had to live without him. Of course, he assured me I would never have to. I just wanted him to know that every time he went away, I really missed him. He's such a big part of my life, so important in every aspect of my life that it's hard to imagine anything without him. It's a wonderful feeling to be so clear about the importance of our relationship, and I feel like the luckiest woman in the world when he says he feels the same way.

So we drove along with the sun slowly setting and the sky filled with streaks of peach, pink and royal blue. It was a perfect time to head to "the point", which was our favorite Lover's Lane before we were married or had kids. It seemed like Larry was in sync with my idea of pretending we were teenagers again.

I couldn't wait until we got there. I knew he would be hard already when we got to the top, just from thinking about it. And I would be ready for him. When he finally pulled into the parking spot, we couldn't keep our hands off each other. We were like two teenagers… and in fact, we hadn't made out in a car since we *were* teenagers.

I unbuttoned Larry's shirt. His kisses tasted so sweet; they had my nipples tingling. I opened my coat again to release my breasts. Larry acted like he had never seen them before as he caressed and sucked my erect nipples.

His touch was exciting me and I wanted him to know it, so I leaned over and unzipped his pants. I stroked his dick. I wanted to put it in my mouth, lick it and savor it like a Popsicle, but first I delicately stroked him with my fingers. I know it was good for him because his kisses became deeper and more intense.

Suddenly I needed to have him inside me. I rose up off the car seat to move my coat out of the way, and plopped back down on the seat with my legs open. Larry moved the seat

104

all the way back and climbed on top of me. He slowly slid his hard dick into me. Just thinking about it gives me goose bumps even now.

He started thrusting... slow at first and then faster, just the way I like it. It was so good; my entire body let go and any tension I had was released all at once. I grabbed Larry's butt and pulled him even further inside me. The feel of his skin and the warmth of his breath on my face made me want him even more. A jolt of electricity shot through me. I was gone, baby, gone. I squeezed my pussy around him and whispered again how much I had missed him. He came, right then, right after me, right there in my arms.

I smiled a sly little smile and whispered, "Welcome, home Sweetie."

~~~

"I like it when a man surprises me with thoughtful gifts or plays little games like leaving a note on my front door. Then I read that note and it tells me to go to another note somewhere else in the house until finally I make it to the bedroom and there he is in bed waiting for me. I think that's sexy."

"A sense of adventure. Cause after awhile if you keep doing the same thing over and over and over, although it's fun to learn the things that turn your partner on, it ends up getting robotic. If every single time he makes you cum within two minutes and you can make him cum within five or whatever, and so you do that every single time, it means nothing after awhile. It's nice to learn, to be able to try new things, or do new things or be in new places."

"I like a guy surprising me with little things... and spontaneity... I dig that."

105

"Probably being able to laugh at himself and being able to have a good time and not take it all so seriously. Sometimes you want to make love, and sometimes you want to have sex... to actually get into it and get down and dirty and be all sweaty. And the idea that you can do that whole range is what makes someone really good in bed."

"I think having sex outside the bedroom and being spontaneous is really important. It spices things up; it makes it more exciting."

"Sex outdoors is excellent, it's great... sometimes even in dangerous places or with a great view."

Gemma's boyfriend Joey was happy to play along when she led him outdoors to her favorite view with an idea to do more than just sightsee...

Gemma & Joey
Getting Caught

My favorite place in this whole city has to be Lookout Mountain. You can see almost 360°. It's absolutely breathtaking. Last week, I took Joey up there for the first time. As we got out of the car, he wrapped his arm around my waist and told me how pretty it was. I lead him toward the stairs and told him he hadn't seen anything yet… the real view was up at the top.

Holding hands, we jogged up the stairs. I pointed out the Hollywood sign to him, excited to share my favorite spot. At the top, I showed him the diagram, turning around and pointing out each location listed on the map. Downtown… Century City… the Hollywood Bowl…. We could see the entire city, and it felt like we were on top of the world.

Joey grinned, happy to see me enjoying myself so much. Standing side by side, his arm around me, we gazed out at the horizon. We were the only ones on top of the mountain and life felt wonderful. I wasn't surprised when Joey gently grabbed my hair and pulled me toward him, planting soft, sweet kisses on my neck.

It was a romantic moment and my body responded. Joey took my face in his hands and pulled me close, kissing my lips. I love his deep sensuous kisses and I melted in his arms, feeling very free. I was so into him and he was wrapped up in the moment. He rubbed my back and massaged my shoulders.

He seemed to forget we were outside in public, because he was getting more and more amorous. He lifted my dress to caress my butt, and to his surprise found that I wasn't wearing any panties! He loved it!

I felt him get hard against me as he planted his hands on my naked cheeks and pulled me against him, his kisses tasting sweeter and sweeter. He ran his hands up and down my thighs. The kissing and rubbing, added to the thrill of doing something naughty outside, drove me crazy.

Joey was really into it. He slipped his hand between my legs and applied pressure with his fingertips. My juices were flowing. His finger slipped inside of me, and oh, I shivered with pleasure. His finger was slipping and sliding against me, and we were both really hot.

Joey gently turned me so my butt was touching his groin, while those magic fingers continued stroking my pussy and rubbing my thighs. I reached back to hold onto him, because I was actually getting dizzy. I could feel the blood pulsing in my veins. Joey kissed me on my neck and my ears and I couldn't help myself. I raised my dress and flashed him a good long look at my bare butt.

He bent down, slid his head under my dress and gently kissed my cheeks. He slipped his fingers between my legs again and stroked my pussy. I drifted off, trembling from the kisses and caresses. I had to hold on to the retaining wall in front of me to get a sense of balance. The wind was blowing through my hair and I felt totally free.

Joey and I were so involved in our sexual escapade that we didn't see or hear the other couple coming up the steps until they made it all the way to the top. I don't know how long they had been standing there when I happened to look back. "Oh, nooo!" was all I could murmur.

Joey saw them too then and quickly stood up. He held me close, laughed, and whispered in my ear that he hoped we were obnoxious enough to make them leave us alone again! He pulled me closer and I could feel how hard he still was.

"It worked; they're leaving," he whispered, and we both laughed. He said we probably sent them running back down those steps in shock, but he didn't care, because it left us alone to finish what we started. He raised the back of my dress and pressed his body into mine as he once again rubbed my butt and thighs. Then he sent those probing fingers back into my pussy. I was definitely still wet and swollen. I knew what he wanted, but I protested lightly. What if someone else came up the steps again? He said he couldn't help it... he couldn't wait any longer. He promised to be quick, and in a flash he unzipped his pants and bent his knees so he could enter me.

Oh, it was so good; I get chills remembering it.

There I was, perched on the edge of the mountaintop, my butt sticking out, overlooking the city and being pleasured by my man. It was absolutely delicious. I remember telling him how naughty he was. But he kept pumping in and out of me and my body locked into his rhythm. He kissed my neck and held my hips as his rhythm and intensity quickened. It was naughty, nasty and breathtaking at the same time.

We bucked against each other as the mountain breeze caressed my cheeks. As much as I was concerned about someone coming up the trail and seeing us, it was too good to stop.

We both moaned and sighed. Every time he entered me he drew me closer. When he pulled out, he slid the tip of his penis over my clit and sent ripples of pleasure through my body. I held him even closer so I could feel more pressure when he entered me. We were slipping and sliding, building intensity. And then we hit it, so big, together. For a moment we were suspended in time and I lost control of my body. The cool breeze, the fresh air, and the warmth of our bodies created the most intense orgasm I've ever had.

It was one of the only times I've had sex outdoors. And one thing I know for sure... I always remember more than just the view when I think about Lookout Mountain.

~~~

"When he attacks me, throws me on the bed and just does me. I love that."

"I love a man who has a passion for life that spills over into sex."

"I really enjoy being sexually aggressive with a man."

"I like when a man takes control of me sexually. But sometimes I like to shake it up and be the one in charge."

Ashley's husband Eric is usually in control. But she enjoys changing roles by occasionally being the one who takes over a lovemaking session...

Ashley & Eric
Slave for Love

Most of the time when we're in the mood to make love, I let Eric lead. But sometimes I like taking control. One night last week, I psyched myself into being a bit of a dominatrix. I wasn't sure how Eric would react, but I thought it would be fun for a change.

We were already becoming aroused, kissing and caressing each other, when I rolled over and straddled him, sitting my butt on his abs. "Come here," I ordered, as I leaned in to kiss him while stroking his nipples.

Teasing him, I rose up onto my knees and caressed my mound while he watched. I ran my fingers through my pussy. Eric couldn't take his eyes off me. I took my time massaging and stimulating myself. He could see my fingers getting wet, and wagged his tongue. I dipped my fingers deeper into my pussy, pulled them out and let him lick them. Then I sat down on his stomach again. Don't rush, I thought.

My legs were spread apart, giving him a good view of my beautiful pussy. Eric tried to touch it. Without saying a word, I brushed his hand away. Then I rose up into a squat position and lowered myself over his cock. Very slowly, I slid up and down against it as it lay on his abdomen. I asked him if he liked it. He nodded and grinned as he reached for my erect nipples. He stroked and flicked them between his fingers while I continued moving against his cock.

Eric became even more excited watching me glide against him. I leaned over and took his nipple into my mouth, and felt his cock go rock hard. The more I sucked the more Eric's body shivered with pleasure. I kissed him and slid my body further up along his chest and then down the entire length of his body. I felt his temperature rise, and presented my nipple to his mouth. He sucked it in, and then moved to the other, taking turns sucking and kissing both of them. I let him enjoy that sensation for a moment and then pulled away. I asked him if he liked that too. He nodded. I planted a lush kiss on his lips and told him he'd get more, *if* he was a good boy.

Opening my legs, I told him to "kiss me right there," pointing to my inner thigh. He got on his knees and licked it instead. I scolded him for not doing exactly as I said, and surprised him by pulling out a little black whip. I flicked it on his ass and told him we'd try again. "Listen up," I demanded, "I want little kisses all the way up my arm this time." He sat up like a good obedient boy and planted soft kisses from my wrist up to my shoulder. I told him that was very good, and he had earned a reward.

"Lay down," I commanded. I climbed on top of him, kissing him while I continued sliding my pussy over his lovely cock. He was ready, so I rose up and squatted over him, sliding my warm hand up and down his cock and aiming it at my pussy. I rubbed the tip of it against my lips and then stopped.

Eric whimpered. I told him he'd have to beg if he wanted more of my sweet stuff. He sat up and assured me that he'd do whatever I wanted if I would please let him have a taste. I made him say "pretty please."

It was difficult not to laugh at his pleading, but I kept a straight face, asking if he was ready to surrender to me. He looked a little puzzled. I asked again, and he very hesitatingly said okay. I had him worried! I told him to close his eyes, and tied a furry blindfold around him. I pulled his legs apart and put a cuff on each ankle and attached them to the corners of the bed. Eric resisted a bit when I reached for his wrists. I whispered, "Do it my way or you get nothing at all." He acquiesced and stuck out his arms. I tied his wrists to the corners of the bed. He was helpless; I could do whatever I wanted.

I pulled out an electric toothbrush and his body tensed when he heard the sound. I gently touched his belly button, moved it to one nipple and then quickly ran it across the fold of his thighs. His cock stood straight up. I rubbed lube on my hands and gently stroked him. Then I stopped doing anything, and let it be silent for a minute. It drove him crazy. He kept asking what was happening… what was I doing?

I could tell he was anxious with anticipation of what was to come. I crawled onto the bed and straddled his body. I took a cool fork and pulled the tines between his legs. He moaned with pleasure. Then I positioned myself over his cock and slid down on top of it. Eric howled with delight as he entered me. I slowly raised and lowered my body onto him… up and down… in and out. He tensed and rocked his body, pushing his cock up into me. He jerked at his restraints and begged to be able to touch me.

But I wasn't ready to let him go yet. I reached down and caressed myself while I was slipping him in and out of me.

The combination of fingers on my clit and Eric's hard cock inside me made me shudder. Eric felt it and moaned again. He wanted closer contact. So I rose up, grabbed his head and slid my mound up to his face so he could smell me. He licked his lips, begging for a taste. Chills ran down my spine at the thought. I hesitated and savored the feeling, then moved closer and presented myself to him. Like a starving man, he licked and sucked my clit. A wave of heat seared through my body.

Even though it was so good, I pulled away again. I removed his blindfold and massaged my clit right in front of his face. He could smell it and he could see it, but he couldn't taste it. His tongue kept reaching out, trying to get some, but I stayed just out of reach. I placed my wet fingers in his mouth and let him have a quick sample. Then I returned to massaging my clit. Again, I let him taste a little and then backed off. Finally, when it seemed like he couldn't stand it anymore, I presented him with my pussy. Oh, he was an eager beaver. "Do it faster… suck it harder," I ordered. He was doing such a good job! Just when I was about to come, I pulled away and teased him that he couldn't have any more. I could see the disappointment in his eyes, but this was too good to let it end so soon.

Running my hands over his body, I felt the tension coursing through him. I slid down, squatted over his hard cock and slipped it into my body again. We were both so ready. Our passion for each other was intense, and after a few deep thrusts, we both came. I had a huge orgasm, and I heard myself yell before I even realized it was coming from me. Eric kept whispering that I was the best… I was incredible. I collapsed onto his chest and we kissed deeply.

We were both quiet for a long moment. After I caught my breath, my smile came back. "So," I whispered, "I guess sometimes you like it when I take charge, don't you?"

~~~

"The way that someone carries themselves, I suppose, is real appealing to me."

"Well, of course he has to be good looking... a nice body and a cute butt."

"I like younger men, but that doesn't necessarily mean that they'll be more sexy than an older man."

"Powerful is what I find sexy."

"I like self-confident, with gentle eyes."

"Good dancer certainly helps."

"Passion."

"I like the eyes, definitely, first and foremost. That's what you notice, they're the windows to the soul."

"Those eyes, and that smile."

"Kissing is sexy. How somebody walks...the way a man walks is very, very sexy to me."

"The smile. And fitness."

"Attitude, confidence."

"Their frankness or honesty. I mean, appearance certainly is a part of it, but it's more the way they carry themselves I think."

"I like to hear him say I love you, because he doesn't say it enough."

"Share their feelings and communicate, because a lot of times miscommunication just ends everything."

"I want him to talk during love making. I want him to say things like how much he wants me, how sexy I am. Things like that."

"Listening to each other. Talking to each other. Finding out what pleases the other. Just communication."

When Sandy openly communicated to her boyfriend Jack exactly what felt best to her, the sex was better for both of them.

Sandy & Jack
Opening Attraction

The last time I made love with my boyfriend Jack, I found out that I can experience the most incredible sex if I just come right out and tell him what I like.

For some reason I had a hard time expressing my desires. Somewhere inside, I felt like I should just let him do what he wanted, and that if I was specific about how I like certain things – how fast, how slow, which position, or the exact area of my clit that felt best – I would seem too experienced and it might put him off.

Once I got over that, and realized that every woman deserves to know her own body, and know it well, the next step was getting up the nerve to communicate with Jack about it.

He had come over to my place to chill out and watch movies. It was raining and cold outside, but my house was toasty and comfortable. I tossed some big soft pillows on the floor in front of the sofa, lit candles all around the room and turned down the lights.

We were going to watch "Pretty Woman", one of my favorite movies, and I wanted to set a romantic mood.

When the doorbell rang, I greeted Jack with a big hug, pulling him inside out of the wet weather. He gave me a lovely kiss. The DVD player had the disc in, ready to go, and Jack had brought over white wine and caramel popcorn – my favorite!

He plopped down on the pillows and leaned back against the sofa, and I wedged myself in front of him so we could cuddle. I like to have my legs rubbed, so I took Jack's hand and stroked it along my thigh. Jack took the hint and caressed me gently. His hands were warm and it felt so relaxing. We kissed, and I sucked on his lower lip before letting it end. That led to another kiss and another kiss. It looked like the movie was going to wait.

Jack likes to explore my body and I love it when he does. We stroked and hugged each other, then slowly undressed. It was cold outside but we were comfortably warm in each other's arms. Jack took his time kissing me, working his way down my body. His tongue circled my nipples until they stood up, and then he gently nipped at them.

I love when he does that, and I told him so, lying back with one arm behind my head, leaving my body open for him to savor. It was a good position to watch him traveling around my body with his mouth, tongue and fingers. I'm very visual, and the sight of him toying with my body like that turned me on big time.

I like the way he starts at the top of my body and slides down, nibbling, sucking and kissing my breasts, belly and thighs. It feels so good, and watching makes me even hotter. When he crawls down between my legs, I reach down and rub his hair or arms. He likes to take his time nuzzling and caressing my pussy.

He slowly made his way back up to my breasts. I arched my back, sticking them out, and he immediately took a nipple into his mouth and sucked. I told him my other nipple was feeling left out, so he took turns moving back and forth between them. It felt great. I told him how good he was making me feel, and he smiled, happy that I liked what he was doing.

I felt really relaxed and quietly said, "I like variety best, baby - a little bit hard and a little soft." Jack responded by caressing my body gently, from my chest to my thighs, then tweaking my nibbles harder than usual. I flinched, but it was great! Then he circled my nipples between his fingers. He never stopped stroking me, even when he looked up to see my response. My smile told him I was enjoying it.

"Kiss me up and down my body again," I said. "I really love that." He immediately slid down my body - planting sweet kisses all the way to my belly, then my inner thighs and on to my knees. When he started to work his way back up my body, I told him I liked the way his kisses tickled my knees, so he lingered there and gave them extra attention.

The more I told him what I liked, the more he enjoyed himself and the more excited he was about making love. He wanted to do me exactly how I wanted it. He was so aroused that he dived between my legs, licking and sucking. I touched his shoulder and asked if he'd give a little love to my inner thighs first, because that's such a sensitive area for me. Ready to please, he slowly moved around, kissing me there just the way I like it. It gave me chills. Then he moved over so he could get back to my clit. I asked him to use a bit of a lighter touch, and he did just what I asked. I could feel the difference immediately. It was amazing and I told him, "That's good, baby, just like that."

Jack was eager to please me; he was really into it. I guess it made me greedy, because I wanted more!

119

I took his hand and put it between my legs, pushing his finger toward the waiting wetness. He knew exactly what I wanted, and slid his finger in and out while he was still nibbling and sucking my clit. Oh, it was incredible!

He thrust his finger in and out of me, faster and faster, while he worked my clit with his tongue. Suddenly, I was over the top! My body jerked and quivered. Jack didn't even come up for air; he just kept licking and sucking as I moaned and held my breath. I had an amazing orgasm. As the last wave of spasms shook me, I was still shoving Jack's head against my pussy.

After I climaxed my body went completely limp. Jack crawled up next to me and gathered me in a soft embrace. "Damn that was good!" he said. I nodded and smiled. Being able to tell my guy exactly what felt best to me, and knowing that it gave him more pleasure too, made it an unforgettable night for both of us.

~~~

"I like a sense of humor. I like warmth and intelligence. And generally, somebody who likes to cuddle."

"I like if they have a quick wit. Of course, they need a serious side as well, but a humorous side is a turn-on for me."

"To me, the two most important things are kindness - meaning a kind-hearted person - and a sense of humor."

Brenda's willingness to respond playfully adds to the fun when her husband Keith decides to spice up breakfast in his own way...

Brenda & Keith
Chocolate Kisses

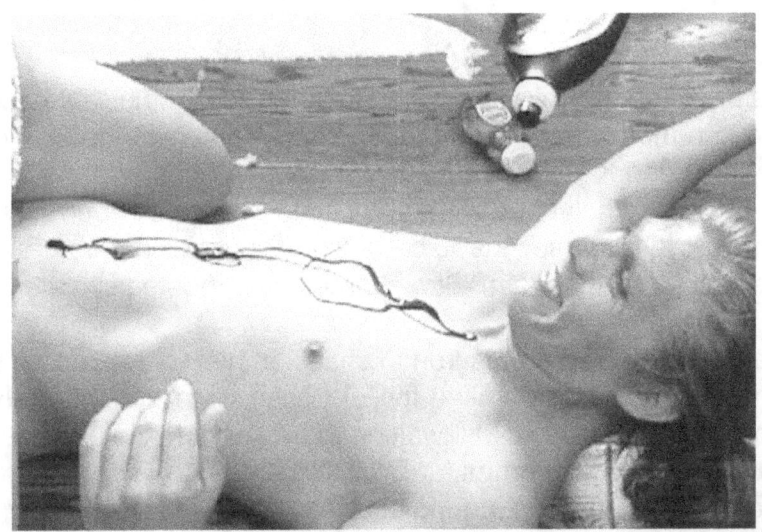

One of my favorite things to do on Saturday is sleep late and read the newspaper in bed. When I'm hungry, I get up and fix something simple for me and my husband Keith.

A few weeks ago, Saturday morning started in that usual way. I was awake and reading the paper, and I thought Keith was downstairs exercising. He yelled up and asked if I could come down. I hesitated, because I wasn't ready to give up my comfortable spot in bed yet. He called to me again, so I forced myself out from under the covers. Tying on my silky nightgown and stepping into my slippers, I padded down the steps to see what was so important.

Keith was waiting for me in the kitchen... with a big surprise! This was not a usual Saturday morning. Cradling a big bowl in his arms, Keith announced he was making me breakfast, and the waffles were almost ready. "What's the occasion?" I asked, and he said no reason, he just wanted to treat me for a change, and he knew how much I loved a homemade breakfast.

121

I was impressed. The aroma of coffee brewing in the pot and waffles baking on the iron was delicious. I pinched a corner off one of the waffles already on the table to steal a taste. It was as good as it smelled.

Keith scooped a big ripe juicy strawberry from the table and fed it to me. When I bit into it, the juice ran down the side of my chin and Keith licked it off. He popped another berry into his own mouth, leaned over, and planted a big strawberry kiss on me. Of course, the juice squirted all over my lips, and Keith licked it off again. Strawberries never tasted sweeter!

Keith lifted the lid on the iron to check on his waffle creations, and the aroma again filled the air. They were perfect, fluffy, golden brown pillows just waiting to be served. He sprinkled blueberries, strawberries, and raspberries on top and finished it off with a generous mound of sweet frothy whipped cream.

Knowing how much I love whipped cream, he devilishly told me to stick out my tongue. He squirted a dollop of the cream onto it. Yum! I slurped and licked my lips, and Keith laid another big kiss on me. It was sweet and warm and messy, and we laughed at each other's sticky faces.

We were just getting started though, because Keith had something unusual in mind. He wanted to serve me up like a waffle! I hadn't realized he was feeling so randy this morning. I tingled with anticipation of where his little game would lead. He lifted me up onto the counter and fed me another pinch of berries and waffles. That's when the real mess began!

I have to admit I've always wanted to smear something gooey on Keith's face, so I shot a scoop of whipped cream into my palm and did just that. But I did it affectionately, and Keith took it in stride. He laughed, even though he was a mess. He retaliated by feeding me a piece of waffle smothered with whipped cream, which got all over me.

I jumped off the counter and tried to get away from him. But Keith caught me around the waist and pulled me to him. I jumped up and clamped my legs around him. He said I was in "big trouble" now, and I told him to bring it on.

He lowered me to the kitchen floor. Kissing me as he untied my bathrobe and undid the buttons on the front of my nightgown, he moved down to my breasts, gently kissing and caressing. I closed my eyes and savored the sensations. I didn't see Keith reach for the chocolate syrup sitting on the counter, but suddenly he rose up, straddled me, flipped the top open and squirted it in on my chest. What a devil! I yelped as the cold syrup hit my warm skin. Keith drew circles around my breasts with it, and then a little chocolate heart on my stomach. He took his time slowly drizzling it on me and called me a sweet chocolate sensation. He said he was hungry and ready for a taste.

He started with my breasts, licking around the chocolate circles and flicking it onto my nipples. He said breakfast had never tasted so good. I was hungry too… wanting more of his tongue. He followed the chocolate trail down my stomach and past my belly button. Oh my! I couldn't have kept my legs closed even if I wanted to!

But I wanted to extend the playtime, so I wiggled away and rolled him over onto his back. It was his turn now. I massaged his chest, moving slowly down to his waist… and then yanked his boxers off! He was not expecting that! I knew exactly what I wanted to do next… so I grabbed the honey bear off the counter and squirted in onto his abs, letting the amber liquid drizzle slowly around his muscles. Now I was ready for a taste, and I savored licking it up and onto his nipples.

I wanted more whipped cream now and I was feeling naughty, so I aimed it at his dick, making a creamy spiral from the base to the tip. It looked like a peppermint stick, and I reminded Keith how much I used to love to suck peppermint sticks.

His eyes rolled back in his head... he knew what was coming and melted at the thought. I don't know what came over me, but I plunged his big-peppermint-stick-dick all the way into my mouth. Usually I don't rush it like that, but this wasn't our usual lovemaking .... and I could tell by Keith's body language that it was working for him!

We were having too much fun to stop so I took one last suck and then sat up on his stomach. By now I was hungry for real. I grabbed a waffle and rubbed it over his chest to coat it with the honey there before I took a bite. Then I rubbed it over my breasts, adding the chocolate that was still covering me to my next bite. Yum. I found the can of whipped cream and squirted that on the waffle for my final bite. I deliberately savored it as Keith watched. And I must say I was pretty proud that I managed to take the edge off my hunger and turn my man on at the same time!

"What about me?" Keith asked. So I squirted a dab of whipped cream onto each of my nipples and said, "Here's yours."

He pulled me close and sucked the cream off my nipples. I felt his dick stiffen against me, as hard as could be. I pulled away and drizzled chocolate over it, then licked him like a Popsicle. Keith moaned with delight. After I licked him clean, I straddled him and gently slid down onto his dick. Moving up and down, I slowed the pace and forgot about the food and the games. I was making love to him now and ready to get serious. But Keith wasn't done yet. He rolled me over onto my back, spread my legs and sprayed a circle of whipped cream around my pussy.

The cold silky texture against my sensitive lips was unexpected... strange but stimulating.

Keith licked the cream off, and kept going, licking my pussy the way he knows I like it. He's so good... I was gyrating with pleasure. He pushed his tongue in and out of me and flicked at my clit. Just when I though I couldn't take any more, he rose up and thrust his dick into me.

Our desire for each other was intense. Keith's muscles strained against me, his thighs tight and his arms cut. He was lost in his own world now, eyes shut as he thrust into me again and again. Then he stopped, gasping for air as he came strong and hard. I groaned in ecstasy, right there with him, as an orgasm rocked my body. We reached our peak together, climaxing in a sweet moment of rapture. A perfect dessert to this unexpected breakfast delight.

Keith dropped back to the floor next to me, exhausted. We laid there against the cool tiles, quiet, catching our breath. Then we looked over at each other and burst out laughing. Wow. What a great start to the weekend. I cuddled up against him and told him he could make me breakfast any time he wanted.

~~~

"They have to be able to talk to me and be able to share things with me and open up to me."

"I like creativity and somebody who can support my creativity."

"It's more the attitude than the actual body, the attitude of being willing to go out and do anything and wanting to experience life. It doesn't matter if it's hiking or bowling or doing something completely ridiculous, as long as they are willing to do it... and a good body type to go along with it... all the better."

Gail and her husband Robert find out the bathtub or shower is a great place to share sexual encounters...

Gail & Robert

Goddess in the Flesh

I love to take showers. Whether it's the soothing warm water inside a beautiful bathroom, or the cool freshness of an uninhibited shower outside at the beach, or the marbled delight of a double showerhead at a tropical resort... I love it all.

Nothing, however, is better than a shower with my husband Robert. He knows it's almost a spiritual thing for me when I'm in there, so he waits while I spend a little time by myself before joining. Even though that's our usual pattern, I'm sometimes drifting off and surprised when he opens the door and slides in behind me.

Robert likes to softly massage me where the water's flowing. I feel like I have the smoothest skin in the world when he runs his hands over me while I'm wet. Added to the warm stream gushing between our bodies, the experience is a real turn on. It makes me feel like a sex goddess.

Sometimes I close my eyes and stand with my back to the water, letting the hot stream pulse against me. Then Robert

126

will rub aromatherapy gel up and down my arms and across my shoulders. Ahhhh.

Last night his big soft hands felt heavenly as he treated me to a firm but slippery massage. I shivered with delight as he kneaded my neck and shoulders, massaging all the tension out of me. Then he slid his hands down and circled my breasts with his fingertips. He smiled and squeezed more shower gel into his hands, rubbing them vigorously to create a creamy white lather.

There's something about the way Robert touches me that sends waves of pleasure straight to my pussy, especially when he massages my breasts. Even in the shower, I could feel my pussy getting wet. I wanted him to feel it too, so I wrapped my leg around his butt. The sensation of my lips touching his thigh woke up his dick, and it came to life between my legs. I smiled and pulled him closer.

He gently turned me around and rested my butt against his groin, exploring every part of my body with his wet, slippery hands. He traced a road map from my pussy to my navel to my nipples. It felt wonderful. I turned back to face him and pulled him in for a kiss under the steamy water. I wrapped my leg around him again, and by the time he slid his thick dick into my warm, wet pussy, I was more than ready to receive him.

We shared a fast, passionate love-making session. We were both so excited, we were ready to come before Robert even entered me. We have since decided that showering together is our very favorite foreplay!

~~~

Many couples also find water play in a Jacuzzi to be erotic, as Bianca and Carl do...

Bianca & Carl
Hot and Hard

Carl always gets home from work before I do, so I wasn't surprised to see the house lit up when I got home last night. I knew he was there, but there was no answer when I called for him. Finally, I found him out back, unwinding in the Jacuzzi.

The drive home from work tends to leave me a little tense, so the Jacuzzi looked like a great idea. I quickly changed into my bathing suit and joined Carl out back. He was sitting on the edge of the Jacuzzi sipping wine. He reached for my hand and helped me step in. The swirling jets of the hot tub started to massage the day's stress right out of me. Carl and I sat with our eyes closed and let the magic bubbles take our tensions away.

After a while, Carl stood up to stretch and then leaned back onto the edge of the tub. His wet skin glistened and I felt an urge to touch him. I slid over between his legs and rose up to kiss his nipples. His penis trembled against me and I knew it wanted some attention. It got bigger and bigger as I massaged it. I moved Carl's swimsuit to the side and knelt in front

128

of him, sliding my hand up and down his shaft. I gave the tip a passionate kiss, and then took the whole thing into my mouth.

Carl's legs tensed and an expression of pure pleasure crossed his face. Smiling, he leaned back, savoring the warmth of my mouth on his dick. His whole body tightened, and I knew that meant he was about to come, so I backed off. I wasn't ready to end this session yet.

Carl slid back down into the water and kissed me, and I wrapped my legs around him. He held me close with one hand and reached for the glass of wine with the other. We both sipped, enjoying the flavor it added to our kisses. Then Carl turned his attention to me.

He caressed my breasts under the warm bubbles, and I closed my eyes and drifted away, my mind filled with erotic images. Carl's fingertips circled my nipples and I tilted my head back and pushed my breasts forward, eager for more.

He read my body language and leaned forward to take my nipple into his mouth while he continued to caress the other one. Then he slid from my nipple, stroked the curves of my breasts, and nibbled on my neck. He gave me a luscious deep kiss and I saw myself as an exotic woman making love to her man.

Suddenly, I felt the urge to have him in me. I wrapped my legs tighter, and he knew what I wanted. He slid his hot shaft between my legs and into my warm, ready pussy. I pumped up and down on him, my breasts bouncing on top of the bubbles. Carl was transfixed by the sight. He moaned softly and closed his eyes, drifting away for a moment. Then he took charge and moved back onto the seat of the Jacuzzi. I straddled him and he kissed me as he slid into me again. Both lost in ecstasy, we pumped in rhythm under the hot bubbling water jets.

Carl's body stiffened and I felt him explode in me. He groaned and grasped me tightly. That put me over the top. I came too, in perfect sync with him. We collapsed against each other, letting the soothing water and the cool evening air bring us back to earth.

After a few minutes, Carl told me he was sure glad I had talked him into getting a Jacuzzi in our yard.

~~~

"I want a man with sensitive hands...someone with an easy touch, as they say."

"I think the most important thing is the daily touches. Reaching out and making that contact. I'm always telling my boyfriend that the hottest thing he does is come up behind me and get his butt, you know, right in the spoon position, only we're standing up."

"I like a man who touches me often. I can never get enough of his hands on me."

Skylar enjoys the spontaneity of sexual arousal when she's least expecting it, or in the middle of a mundane chore...

130

Skylar & Josh
Impulsive Action

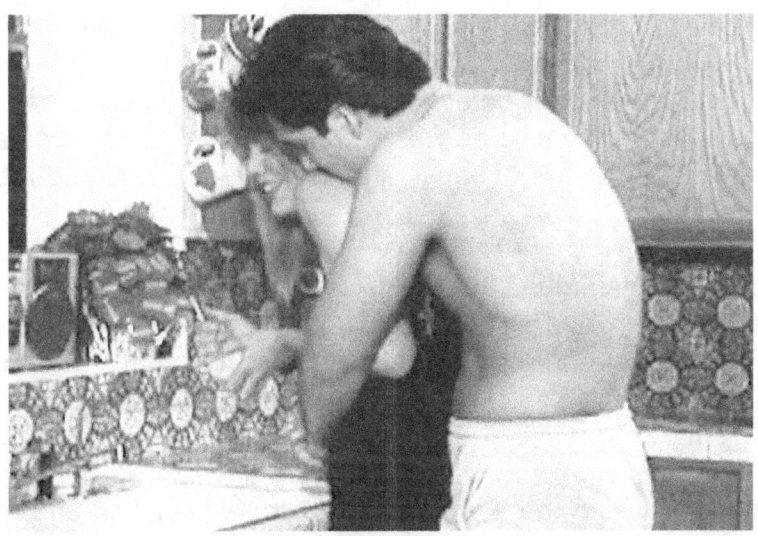

Cooking is boring to me if it gets too routine. But my guy is full of surprises, and he can make anything fun. I chuckle thinking about some of the things that turn him on and make him have to reach out and touch me.

One evening, I was standing in the kitchen peeling potatoes and heard Josh come in behind me. He was grinning and wearing only his boxers. He told me I looked really good "working that peeler." All I could do was laugh. I'm very lucky... because he tells me I look good doing something almost every day. Sometimes he says it when he's on his way out... or when I'm on my way out. But tonight, in his boxers, I knew it was a prelude.

He snuggled up behind me, wrapping his arms around my waist and pulling my backside into his groin. I told him I never get tired of hearing him tell me I look good. He nuzzled his face into the back of my neck, gently caressing up and down the sides of my body while I struggled to continue peeling potatoes. He pulled me tighter into his body and I told him I'd never be

131

able to make dinner if he kept distracting me that way! He whispered that he wouldn't mind delaying dinner a bit. I wondered what had gotten into him, because he's always hungry and always ready to eat.

I picked up another potato. Josh slid his hands down to my inner thighs. He said he was starved, but not for dinner... all he wanted was me. That sent a shiver through me and I felt myself flush.

Josh held me around the waist, kissing my ear lobe. I leaned back into him, and it was a soothing, sexy feeling. I asked him if he'd kiss the back of my neck... I love how that feels. His warm breath and soft kisses on my nape made me melt back into him.

He kept kissing me there while he stroked my butt and my belly. He slowly pushed my skirt up along my thigh, and when he discovered I wasn't wearing any panties, his dick went instant-hard! He knelt and kissed my naked cheeks, and I had to lean on the sink for support because he made me weak in the knees. He licked his finger and slid it into my pussy. My body flushed and I flashed hot all over. Believe it or not, I was still trying to peel potatoes, working on auto-pilot.

He asked me what I was thinking about, and I told him I wasn't thinking about anything at all... except him. He stood up, without his boxers, and placed his knees between my legs. In one smooth move, he parted my legs, pulled me into him and slid his big dick into me. I had to grab onto the sink with both hands. My body was one with him as he slowly began to thrust.

I hung onto the kitchen counter, sticking my butt out toward him so he could plunge even deeper inside me. He held me by the waist with one hand, his other traveling up and down my back as he pumped. The sensation was incredible.

132

I responded by pumping back against him even harder. All thoughts of cooking or potatoes had fled my mind!

I leaned further over the sink, absorbing the force of his thrusts. An intense shiver rippled through my body. He pushed my hair to the side and grabbed my shoulders, kissing my neck while he was plunged deep inside me. I was so turned on and close to a huge orgasm. He pulled me to him, as close as he could get me. My body trembled. The orgasm crashed through me like a giant wave, making me yell. It was intense, and I shuddered deep inside. That was all it took for Josh. His body stiffened and he clung to me as he came too.

We slumped against the sink. Before I could even catch my breath, Josh whispered in my ear that he loved tonight's menu.

~~~

"A good kiss can just drive me up the wall, completely."

"It's in his kiss. For me, absolutely. I want a good kisser."

"To be kissed a lot, that's what I want... kissing more than the actual act itself. A lot of women enjoy foreplay more than they enjoy the actual act. Men want to get right to the sex, but I think women like to take it slower."

"Sometimes I like to seduce my husband. Better me than somebody else, right?"

"I like when he has an erection in public... I like how it feels."

"I get a kick out of surprising my guy with sex in dangerous places. He loves it."

Vanessa finds that an unexpected location is sometimes all it takes for an amorous adventure to start...

Vanessa & Peter

Raw Exposure

Our new home has a beautiful back yard filled with luscious tropical bushes, plants and trees. My new favorite thing is to find a few minutes to chill out there on the lounge chair, magazine in hand and a drink close by. It's heaven. My son J.J. is a toddler now, so most of my time is spent running after him. But everyday I try to take a break outside, usually when he's napping.

I have a fairly secluded yard, although I have found that my neighbor Mr. Carson can look down into it if he's sitting on his upstairs deck. Generally, I can tell if he's up there; he'll make some kind of noise, out of courtesy I think, to announce his presence. He's a kind gentleman in his 60's and in good health, and we've invited him to a few backyard barbeques.

The neighbors on the other side of the fence, The Goldmans, are in their 40's and pretty lively. If I'm outside sitting under my palm tree, their bedroom window is right next to me. I don't mean to snoop, but I do hear them sometimes, so I know they are quite sexually active.

Anyway, the past week had been extremely busy for me. Peter worked late every night and the baby was getting stronger at walking, so he was into everything. I had just finished feeding him lunch one day when in walked Peter. He had finished his project at work and decided to come home early. Wonderful news, because it was unusual to see him on a weekday afternoon. He offered to put the baby down for his nap, and I jumped at the chance for some quiet time. Grabbing a magazine and a soft drink, I settled down on my lounge chair in the yard. Peter joined me a little while later after the baby was asleep for some rare free time alone.

Peter looked so sexy - he had changed into shorts and his shirt was unbuttoned, revealing his pecs. I grabbed his collar, pulled him close and gave him a big kiss. I felt him start to relax. I slid my hand under his shirt and massaged his chest. My fingers went straight to his nipples. Then on impulse, I drifted down to his pants, unzipped them and pulled his dick out, right there in the yard. Peter has great equipment, and I love feeling it grow in my hand.

I bent over to kiss the tip and greedy me, I had to have it all. I slipped him deep into my mouth. I love giving head to Peter, and of course he is a willing receiver. He stood up and wobbled as he shook off his shorts, stepping out of his sandals while he was still in my mouth. As I pleasured him, I thought I saw movement out of the corner of my eye. But nobody was in the yard except us, so I didn't give it a second thought.

Peter guided me back onto the lounge chair and licked his finger, dipping it into my pussy. It was wet and slippery when he pulled it out. He stroked my clit, slowly at first and then with more pressure. My juices flowed as he continued to pump his finger in and out, only stopping to massage my clit.

Making love outside under the sun felt so good. Peter was licking my pussy now and his tongue was so good I felt like yelling. I managed to keep it down to a moan.

Peter changed position and faced my pussy while kneeling in front of me. He spread my legs and licked his lips before diving in again. His skillful tongue was warm and wet, and within minutes I was deep inside my ecstasy zone. Eyes closed, enjoying the ride, I forgot everything except Peter and his talented tongue. When I opened my eyes, I saw Mr. Carson sitting on his deck, a sly smile on his face. But just then Peter's tongue hit my spot again and I wasn't aware of anything except the heat that was like sunshine bursting through me. It was brilliant.

Suddenly, without warning, Peter rose up on his knees and drove his huge dick into me. I was more than ready for him. I grabbed his butt and pulled him deep inside. In and out, in and out, the friction drove me crazy. Each time he thrust into me, I rose up to meet him.

I tilted my head back, caught up in the ecstasy, and this time I was sure. There was Mr. Carson, sitting in his chair smiling, his hand resting on his groin. I didn't even care; I was too overwhelmed by Peter's sexual prowess. This was so good... too good to let anything get in the way.

Peter lifted one of my legs and rested it on his shoulder so he could go even deeper. He leaned over me like he was doing push-ups. The position forced pressure on my clit and it was wonderful. After a few more strokes, I placed my other leg on his shoulder and gave Peter total access to my pussy.

We rocked so wildly that I started slipping off the lounge chair! As I wiggled to scoot myself back onto it, I saw Mr. Carson was still there. He was leaning over his balcony trying to see us better, holding his dick in his hand. I whispered to Peter that Old Mr. Carson was watching us, but Peter wasn't thrown for even a moment. He just whispered, "Then let's finish the show for him."

He climbed up next to me and we kissed deeply. His hand moved back down to massage my clit and his sweet lips sucked my nipples. That drives me absolutely crazy. Once again Peter entered my eager body and we made love like it was the first time.

I felt him explode inside me, like a burst of heat from a volcano. His back arched and my muscles contracted, gripping on to him. My body couldn't wait another moment and I came too, hard, joining with him even as I remained lost in my own world. Peter was moaning and whispering that it was so good... so good. We collapsed back onto the lounge chair, breathing heavily and completely satisfied.

As for Old Mr. Carson, when I opened my eyes and looked up, he was gone. But now that we were lying there, so quiet, we got the real surprise of the day. Drifting from the next door window we heard our other neighbor moaning, "Now lick the whipped cream off me."

All Peter and I could do was laugh. There must have been something in the air that afternoon. Everybody in our neighborhood was in a sexy mood.

~~~

"Women want men to take their time in bed. And they want to be asked: what do you like?"

"I like a man who is sensitive to my needs."

Next, Carmen experiences female ejaculation, something that sex researchers have only recently discovered and put a name to.

Carmen & Emilio
Naked Desire

I love to run. I love the wind whipping through my hair and the smell of the fresh air, so I work hard to include jogging in my schedule as many days as possible. For the past six months, I've been jogging alone on Monday, Wednesday, and Friday. On Saturdays, my boyfriend Emilio comes too. We meet at the park and run along the river's edge for two miles, then turn and jog back to my place. It's a challenging 4 -1/2 miles, and Emilio can't keep up with me.

I get back to my apartment first. Generally I'm naked and in the shower by the time he gets there, my adrenalin still flowing from the brisk run. Last Saturday, I had just finished washing my hair and stepped out of the shower when Emilio stepped in. I dried myself off and slathered on body oil as he soaped up. Still tingling from the jog, I wrapped a towel around my wet hair and another around my body as Emilio stepped out of the shower.

Leaving him to dry off, I went to the bedroom and stretched

138

out on the bed. My muscles were taut and tired and it felt so good to be prone. A few minutes later, Emilio plopped down on his stomach next to me. He looked so cute, all clean and naked. I got aroused right away. I opened the bottom of my towel and flashed him, suggestively rubbing my hand over my thighs. Emilio was on me in a flash.

I leaned back onto the pillow and he climbed up to kiss me, working his way from my neck to my lips. I was ready for whatever he had in mind, so I threw off my towel completely. Emilio rose up on his knees and nuzzled my belly button. He gently unwrapped the towel from my hair and nibbled on my ears. Moving lower, he gave my nipples some welcome attention, sucking and gently squeezing them. He went back and forth, sucking one and tweaking the other. The nipple play aroused me even more. My body was hungry for him.

Raising my knees, I opened my legs and gently pushed his head lower. Emilio followed my cue and kissed my stomach. Just thinking about what was coming next made me shudder.

I drew my legs up, resting my toes on his shoulders. Emilio kissed my pussy, and I felt his warm breath on my thighs. I trembled at the sensation. His fingers slowly parted my lips, and then he gently licked my folds. Applying more and more pressure, he started sucking and licking and telling me how good I tasted.

When Emilio lets me know how much he enjoys pleasuring me, it makes it even better. He's really good about verbalizing what he feels, and that's part of why our sex life is so good. We've gotten to know each other's bodies really well, but we still talk freely about sex and tell each other how much we enjoy our love making.

He was saying how sweet I tasted, and I tingled with anticipation. I wanted him to hit my spot hard, and I told him so. He

139

nuzzled his face between my legs and slid the tip of his nose up to my clit. Then he wrapped his lips around my clit and sucked hard. He slid to my opening and sucked there too. The feeling was intense.

He paused for a moment and I reassured him that what he was doing felt great. He asked me to show him exactly how I wanted it, so I took his hand and placed it over my clit, pressing real hard. He got the idea and put two of his fingers on me, pressing up and down quickly and firmly. He wet one of them, plunging it deep inside me, and then rubbed the wetness all around my clit. I loved it. My body responded to him, moving along with his rhythm.

He continued to stroke against my wet clit while he thrust his finger in and out. My mind exploded in a kaleidoscope of colors. "Do it hard and fast now, baby, slam it! Slam it in and out. You know if you do it right I'll squirt when I come."

The air was thick with sexual tension. My body was super sensitive; all my nerve endings charged. Emilio was wonderful, his finger sliding in and out while he kept pressure on my clit - up and down and all around it. He licked my pussy and nibbled on my clit, gently pulling it through his teeth. I'm the kind of woman who likes that amount of pressure... it feels really good to me. We've talked about it so Emilio knows I can take it.

I looked up and watched him doing me, and the sight sent a chill through my body. I knew I was coming and I moaned, "Here I come, baby... here I come."

My body tensed. I flashed hot all over and a long wail escaped my lips. Emilio raised his head and smiled. My body was still convulsing and I could hardly talk. I was deep in the zone. I squirted more than once.

140

"Look," I showed him, "Look what you've done to me." I pulled him close and told him he was magnificent. My man knows how to do me right.

~~~

"We love to play pick up. I pretend I don't even know Steve. Then I meet him some place and convince him to go home with me."

"I've had three-ways with two men a few times. And it was great, it was great. It basically depends on the partner, or partners."

"I'm somewhat adventuresome. But there are places where I draw the line. I'm not willing to bring another woman into my bedroom with my man. I guess I'm just too selfish and jealous for that. It would make me crazy if he showed too much attention to her and not enough to me. I'd go nuts."

"I've never considered having sex with two men but I don't mind talking about it in the bedroom. I think exchanging fantasies or sharing them can spice things up a lot."

Being open and understanding about fantasies lead to great sex for Christina and Troy…

Christina & Troy
Me in the Middle

My friend Gina and I have been really close for many years. We've shared lots of good times, and stories about some of our intimate moments.

Last week after we met for lunch, I had a good story to tell Gina. "You'll never guess what Troy and I did last weekend," I teased her. "I don't want to guess," Gina said, "just tell me." She was all ears and I was dying to tell her about my latest sexual adventure.

She ordered a cup of coffee and said she wanted all the details. "Well," I started, "Troy's sister offered us her cabin up at Big Bear for the weekend. So we made plans to drive up Friday night and come back Sunday evening. Troy and I have both been really busy, and we were looking forward to a few days away from the usual routine."

I spun the tale out for her, exactly as it happened.

On the way up, Troy and I got into a conversation about sexual fantasies. That's an area we haven't explored very much, and he was curious about what goes on inside my head. He asked if I had any sexual fantasies I wanted to share. I was hesitant, wondering why he asked... what made him curious now? He said he wanted to know what turned me on because he'd read it could add a little spice to our lovemaking.

I was intrigued, but I told him nothing specific came into my mind. He said he didn't want me to shut him out, so I promised I would think about it and we could talk more when we got to the cabin. I wasn't telling him the complete truth, but I wasn't sure how I felt about revealing the fact that I was fantasizing about other men!

When we arrived at Big Bear, we unpacked and decided to have a drink and chill out in the Jacuzzi. It's a beautiful place. The cabin sits on a ridge overlooking the valley and the view from the backyard makes you feel like you're on your own private island. It was a warm summer day, the perfect opportunity to go topless, so I went for it. I eased into the bubbling water and Troy brought the drinks out and got in with me.

We sat for a moment with our eyes closed, relaxing and enjoying the quiet. The bubbles rippled across my nipples, and before long they were erect. They looked enormous in the water. It made me think about making love. I had forgotten that Troy was sitting across from me, watching me with a smile on his face. I think he read my mind! He urged me to come out with it and tell him what I fantasized about. I smiled and asked if he was sure he wanted to know. He assured me he did, moving over to sit next to me. He kissed me softly on the lips and caressed my breasts.

Slowly and hesitantly, I opened up to him. I told him that lately I had been fantasizing about "juicy sex"... you know, the kind that has you dripping before a man even gets inside you.

The kind of sex you read about in a good trashy romance novel. I said that when I visualize one of those scenes, the guys are always tall and muscular and we're doing forbidden things. He listened intently and wanted to hear more. He wanted to know just what I saw myself doing with those muscular guys... what kind of forbidden things?

That threw me off balance. It was hard enough to give him my intimate thoughts in broad strokes, and I was uneasy talking to him in detail. I tried to change the subject. Mostly, I didn't want to talk about other men and risk it sounding like I was searching for a new partner.

But Troy was intent on getting an answer. He wanted me to describe what I would do with my dream lover. It was hard getting the words out, but I tried. "Maybe he would rub my back for a while," I told Troy. "And massage me. I don't know. And you'd be there too, of course, kissing me while he was rubbing my back. "

"Oh....," he said, intrigued, "so there are three of us?" "Yeah," I answered hesitantly, "sometimes."

Troy kissed me. As if he wanted to play out the fantasy, he asked me to picture exactly what I had just told him... my "dream lover" was rubbing my back, and Troy was here too, kissing me. The thought was very arousing, and I could actually feel another man's hands on me while Troy and I kissed!

He took my drink from me and sat it on the deck. Then he pulled me close and hugged me. Holding me tight, he asked what else I would be doing in my fantasy. I still didn't feel completely safe opening up. I was embarrassed. But Troy prodded, asking if the next thing I pictured in my fantasy was going down on the guy.

I didn't have a clear answer. I was treading lightly because

I didn't want to hurt his feelings by admitting I did sometimes picture another man joining us. Troy kept caressing my breasts as we talked and I flashed in and out of my fantasy. I told him that he was the most important thing to me, more important than any kind of fantasy. I told him I had to know he was really comfortable with me talking about this before I could go any further. I didn't want anything – especially something not real – to come between us.

Troy leaned over and sucked my nipple into his mouth. The warmth of his tongue was comforting. He slid his hand down my abdomen, rubbing gently. His fingers slipped under my bikini bottom and down between my legs. I licked my lips, closed my eyes and tilted my head back. Troy continued caressing me and my mind drifted off to a sensuous haze of temptations. He asked me to go with it... to let myself slip away into my favorite fantasy and not hold anything back.

The water in the Jacuzzi bubbled and the steam rose in a misty fog. Troy kissed me, slowly moving down to my breasts and then back up to my neck. He nibbled on my earlobe and licked the top of my ear. My body shuddered.

My mind filled with images of our friend Dexter. Dexter is a beautiful black man who stands 6'6" and has a gorgeous physique. He isn't a body builder but he's cut like one... his broad chest perfectly balanced atop his chiseled waist. His pecs are prominent and in perfect proportion to his buffed biceps. There isn't an ounce of fat on him.

Dexter worked with Troy and had joined us for dinner on several occasions. I was intrigued by him and wanted to get to know him better. There's a mystique about him, and I had found myself imagining what it would be like to have him make love to me. I became obsessed with the idea of feeling his muscular body entwined with mine. I don't know what got into me up at the cabin, sitting in the hot tub with Troy, but suddenly all I could think about was having sex with Dexter.

I didn't have the nerve to ask about having Dexter actually join us - and I wasn't sure I *wanted* him to actually join us - but he was here now, in my fantasy. I pictured myself sitting between Troy, my love, and Dexter, my new infatuation. The thought of having two men focus all their attention on wanting to please me was a mind-blowing experience.

For just a moment, my mind stopped and I opened my eyes. Troy was getting on his knees in front of me. I laid my head back on the edge of the deck. My imagination took off again: Dexter lifted my butt and sat me on his lap. He whispered that he'd always had a crush on me. Troy moved closer and kissed my belly button underwater, slowly working his way up to my breasts. He licked each one softly and sucked firmly on my nipples.

My pussy throbbed. I felt Dexter's breath on my shoulder. He slid his hands around my waist. His cheek touched mine and I turned my head toward him. His thick, tender lips enveloped my mouth and his soft tongue played with mine, circling and probing. He sucked the edge of my lips and then plunged his tongue deep into my mouth. I caught his tongue between my teeth and gently pulled. I could tell Dexter wanted me; his dick was hard and rising, contacting my pussy as we kissed.

I raised my leg to get into a better position. As I opened my eyes in the real world, Troy lifted me out of the water and laid me on the deck. Kneeling on the Jacuzzi step, he spread my legs open, pulled my bikini bottom aside and plunged his tongue into me. He began to lick and suck my pussy like it was the first time he'd ever tasted me. The more he sucked and licked, the wetter I got. I told him I really *really* liked what he was doing to me.

I closed my eyes and went back to Dexter. He and Troy took

turns going down on me.

I closed my eyes and went back to Dexter. He and Troy took turns going down on me. Dexter lifted his head, telling me he loved my taste. It was a mind-blowing experience and I let myself sink into it. The licking and sucking came to a gradual halt, and Dexter and Troy were now standing in the Jacuzzi. They were both naked and their dicks were rock hard and at full mast. They each held out a hand to lead me back into the water. I stepped in, turned around, and pushed Troy back onto the bench. I bent over in front of him and put my mouth on his big hard dick. He tilted his head back onto the deck, his expression ecstatic.

Dexter knelt behind me. He caressed my butt, kissing my cheeks and savoring my pussy. He took my breast in one hand and slid the fingers of his other hand onto my clit, massaging gently. It made me suck Troy's dick even faster, pulling him deeper into my mouth. I was very excited and my pussy was throbbing. Dexter leaned into me doggy-style; I felt his dick resting at the edge of my opening. He pushed into me, slowly and gently, but still I knew I had never had anything that big inside of me before. He pressed in a little more, and then slowly pulled out. Then he plunged in further still, and slid out again. I was speechless, he felt so good.

I gripped Troy's dick in my mouth while I thrust my butt up to connect with Dexter's big dick. My body quivered as he thrust all the way into me. It was intense... I was seeing stars, but I wanted to feel him deeper and deeper inside me. My entire body shivered.

Trembling, I opened my eyes, back to reality, and watched Troy sucking my pussy. I grabbed his hair and pressed him into me, hard. I moaned, as sensation shot through my body. I closed my eyes and sank back into my fantasy.

I was tingling from head to toe with the pleasure of having two men savor my body. They each had a breast in their mouth now. Troy was stroking my clit as Dexter plunged his fingers in and out of my pussy. Their hands were soft and gentle and every nerve in my body reacted. Now it was Troy's turn. He picked me up and turned me around to straddle him, sliding me down onto his dick. Dexter moved behind me, his dick pushing between my legs. He eased his hand between us and found my clit. The moment he touched it, I moaned in ecstasy. Dexter massaged it as Troy thrust into my pussy. My entire body was on fire. I felt like I was going to explode. This was the best sex I'd ever had... real or not.

I could barely catch my breath. I opened my eyes, and Troy asked if I was having fun. I sure was. I closed my eyes again to finish my fantasy threesome session.

In my mind, Dexter had moved to the edge of the Jacuzzi, where he sat stroking himself. He asked if I wanted some. I grinned and leaned over, licking it like a lollipop. I was tempted to see if I could get the whole thing in my mouth. As I slid my lips up and down on Dexter's dick, Troy's dick slid deeper into my fevered body. An involuntary spasm shook me. Dexter got even more excited by my reaction, and I could tell that he was close to coming.

Troy reached around and slapped my butt. The sensation was pleasantly painful. My nipples stood at attention and my pussy started to contract. Troy grew bigger and harder than ever, and climaxed inside me with a loud groan. Then he pulled out and Dexter stepped in, picking me up and sliding into my dripping pussy. The size of his dick and the beauty of his black skin drove me crazy. We moved in perfect rhythm as he thrust harder and deeper. I screamed with joy as Dexter's body stiffened. He exploded inside me and my orgasm rolled through my entire body.

We fell limp into each other's arms.

After one last tremor, I awoke from my beautiful haze. Troy's limp body was on top of me. He rolled over onto the deck. I reached for him, and he gently stroked my arm.

He said he felt incredible. I smiled and said I was glad he asked me about my fantasies. He said if it was always gonna be that good, he planned on asking me about them more often.

That was the end of the story. When I finished, my friend Gina wanted to know if I was making the whole thing up. True story, I told her. Every last word. And it was some of the best sex Troy and I had ever had.

Gina didn't have much to say. She just smiled and said she intended to explore her own fantasies a bit more. She predicted that the next we saw each other, she would have her own great story to tell me!

~~~

"I really like it when my husband pays attention to me. I like an equal amount of attention to be on what he wants, and on what I want."

"I need a man who knows how to use his body efficiently to make his partner happy."

"I like it when Ted shampoos my hair."

"There's nothing sexier than getting physical in a shower or bathtub."

"When Shawn and I bathe together, it's very romantic for me. We always light candles and it's so relaxing; we sit in the hot bath and add some oils and let ourselves have that time together."

"I can usually tell a good lover by the way he dances."

"A guy better know how to do my G-spot."

"We're all different, and for me, the G-spot doesn't do too much. My boyfriend knows where it is and he stimulates it every once in a while, but for me, I'm very clitoral-oriented."

"I know that supposedly everyone has a G-spot. Some of us just don't know where the heck it is."

"Two men at one time? I don't know, maybe."

"Yeah, of course I've thought about a three-way. I think everybody has."

"I'm married. He probably wouldn't go for it. Actually, I'm pretty sure he definitely wouldn't go for it!"

"Yes, I have experienced a three-way. And I felt really crowded. Because I felt like all the attention was on me and it was too goddess-like for me to handle. I'd rather have a one-on-one where you can experience the give and the take without everyone trying to give to you and you feeling crowded."

"A three-way? Well, not with another woman. Maybe with another man if my husband was okay about it. It would depend on the situation and how comfortable everybody was with one another. And definitely it would depend on how comfortable my husband would be with it, you know, because ultimately that would affect our relationship."

150

"I love the attention that my man gives me and the desire that you can see in his eyes. Him really wanting to be there with me is the biggest turn-on of all."

~~~

We hope you've enjoyed these stories from the minds of real couples.

Share sexual secrets with your partner and everything in your relationship will be better.

Exclusive
Free DVD Offer!

Details at www.lovingsex.com/ssee

The Alexander Institute produces the most critically acclaimed sexuality video series for couples and singles who want to enhance their sex lives. Loving Sex is our tastefully explicit series of over 40 erotic programs for lovers who desire incredible sex. Video versions of most of the scenarios in this book are included on the DVDs "What Women Want," "What Men Want," "More of What Women Want" and "More of What Men Want."

Real Couples, Real Sex, Real Life

Survey Form

Your opinion is very important to us. Complete this survey form, and we'll give you one FREE DVD of your choice with each additional DVD you order using this form.

Please answer all of the questions below:	Yes	Not sure	No
1. I got this product to learn about sexuality	☐	☐	☐
2. I got this product to be aroused	☐	☐	☐
After enjoying this product:			
3. I learned something new about sexuality	☐	☐	☐
4. My sexuality communication skills are better	☐	☐	☐
5. My sex life is better	☐	☐	☐
6. I'd recommend this product to friends	☐	☐	☐
7. I'd buy more products from this series	☐	☐	☐
8. Sexuality products like this one are helpful	☐	☐	☐

9. I'm Male ☐   Female ☐   9A. Currently married Yes ☐   No ☐
10. If unmarried, I'm in a committed intimate relationship   Yes ☐   No ☐
11. I enjoyed this product with my partner   Yes ☐   No ☐
12. My age group is   21-35 ☐   36-50 ☐   51+ ☐
13. I watch explicit programs   often ☐   rarely ☐   never ☐

To complete this survey online and to check out our latest special deals go to www.lovingsex.com/ns

Select your buy 1 get 1 free deal   **Please fill in the DVD item numbers below**

Buy 1 DVD get 1 FREE   **$19.95** ☐   Paid DVD _____   FREE DVD _____

Buy 2 DVDs get 2 FREE   **$39.95** ☐   Paid DVD _____   FREE DVD _____

Buy 3 DVDs get 3 FREE   **$59.95** ☐   Paid DVD _____   FREE DVD _____

For additional FREE DVDs, list on separate paper each additional DVD
you order for $19.95 and the additional FREE DVD(s) you want.

DB401 - Yoga book & DVD	$45 $15 ☐	SE9732 - Romeo G-Spot Vibe	$27 $16 ☐
DB650 - Erotic Stories Book w/DVD	$72 $12 ☐	SE0782 - Butterfly Kiss Vibe	$15 $12 ☐
DB691 - Bondage Book w/DVD	$35 $10 ☐	SE2958 - Nick Hawk Penis Pump	$30 $24 ☐
DT657 - Endless Shades Kit	$80 $26 ☐	T101 - 10" Wand Massager	$65 $45 ☐
BT003 - Prince Charming	$20 $10 ☐	*Luxury* SE0610 - Jack Rabbit	$76 $56 ☐
TPM02 - Joli Black ☐ White ☐	$15 $6 ☐	*Luxury* T103 - G-Vibe	$99 $79 ☐
BT006 - Lipstick Black ☐ Silver ☐	$25 $9 ☐	*Luxury* T105 - LEAF Vitality	$110 $79 ☐
BT301 - Lube $8 $4 ☐ BT302 - Oil $8 $4 ☐		*Luxury* T106 - Lelo Soraya	$190 $139 ☐
SE9709 - Anastasia's Kegel Balls	$24 $16 ☐	*Luxury* T107 - We-Vibe 2	$80 $64 ☐
SE9730 - Athena Multi-Head Vibe	$10 $8 ☐	*Luxury* T108 - We-Vibe 4	$160 $119 ☐

Total $_____

California residents please add 9% sales tax $_____

Must add S&H ☐ $6.95 for regular mail ☐ $9.95 for priority mail or to Canada $_____

TOTAL enclosed **(U.S. Dollars, no Canadian Dollars)** $_____

Credit card # _____ Exp. _____

Signature _____ Date _____ Security code _____

I certify that I'm over 21. Payment in U.S. Dollars only. Valid only in the U.S. and Canada.

Name _____

Address _____

City _____ State _____ Zip _____

Phone _____ Email _____

Your data is always safe with us. We never give, trade or sell any data to anyone!

Mail this survey form with payment to: Alexander Institute, Inc.
15124 Ventura Blvd., Suite 206, Sherman Oaks, CA 91403, U.S.A.

The world's largest sex education series

Loving Sex

New for 2014

D658	D659
Sex Games for Couples	Body-to-Body Nuru Massage

Advanced Sex Positions

D844	D845	D618	D619
Seductive Sex Positions	Erotic Sex Positions	101 Advanced Sex Positions 1	101 Advanced Sex Positions 2

Bondage Play

D657	D629
Endless Shades of Great Sex	Erotic Spanking and Bondage

What Men & Women Want

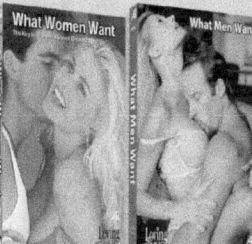

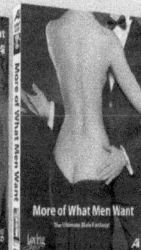

D602	D606	D603	D607
What Women Want	What Men Want	More of What Women Want	More of What Men Want

Group Sex

D651	D653
Swinging Lovers	Great Sex for 3

Eastern Sex Secrets

D650	D648	D647	D645
The Tao of Great Sex	Sex Secrets of Modern Geisha	Thai Massage for Lovers	Erotic Yoga for Couples

Ranked the Best by Men's Health Magazine

Her Sexual Secrets

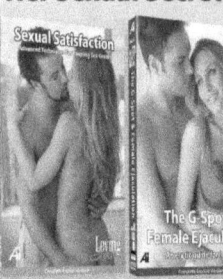 

D613	D641
Sexual Satisfaction	G-Spot & Female Ejaculation

Juli Ashton's Sexuality Reports

D610	D612	D608	D611
Sex Around the House	Toys for Great Sex	Swinging	Erotic Seduction

Never Too Old for Sex

D623	D624	D640
Great Sex Over 50 for Men	Great Sex Over 50 for Women	Sexual Healing

Amazing Orgasms

 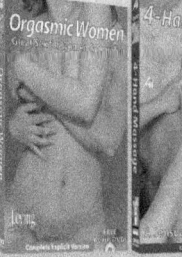

D649	D654	D652
101 Masturbation Secrets for Lovers	Orgasmic Women	4-Hand Massage

Tantric Sex

 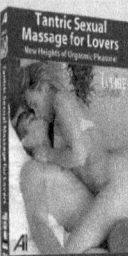

D617	D625	D626
The Modern Tantra	Tantric Sexual Massage	Advanced Tantric Sex Secrets

The Modern Kama Sutra

 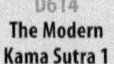  

D614	D615	D616
The Modern Kama Sutra 1	The Modern Kama Sutra 2	The Modern Kama Sutra 3

For our latest deals go to www.lovingsex.com/ns

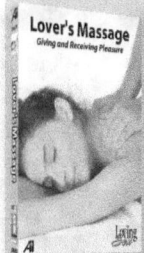   

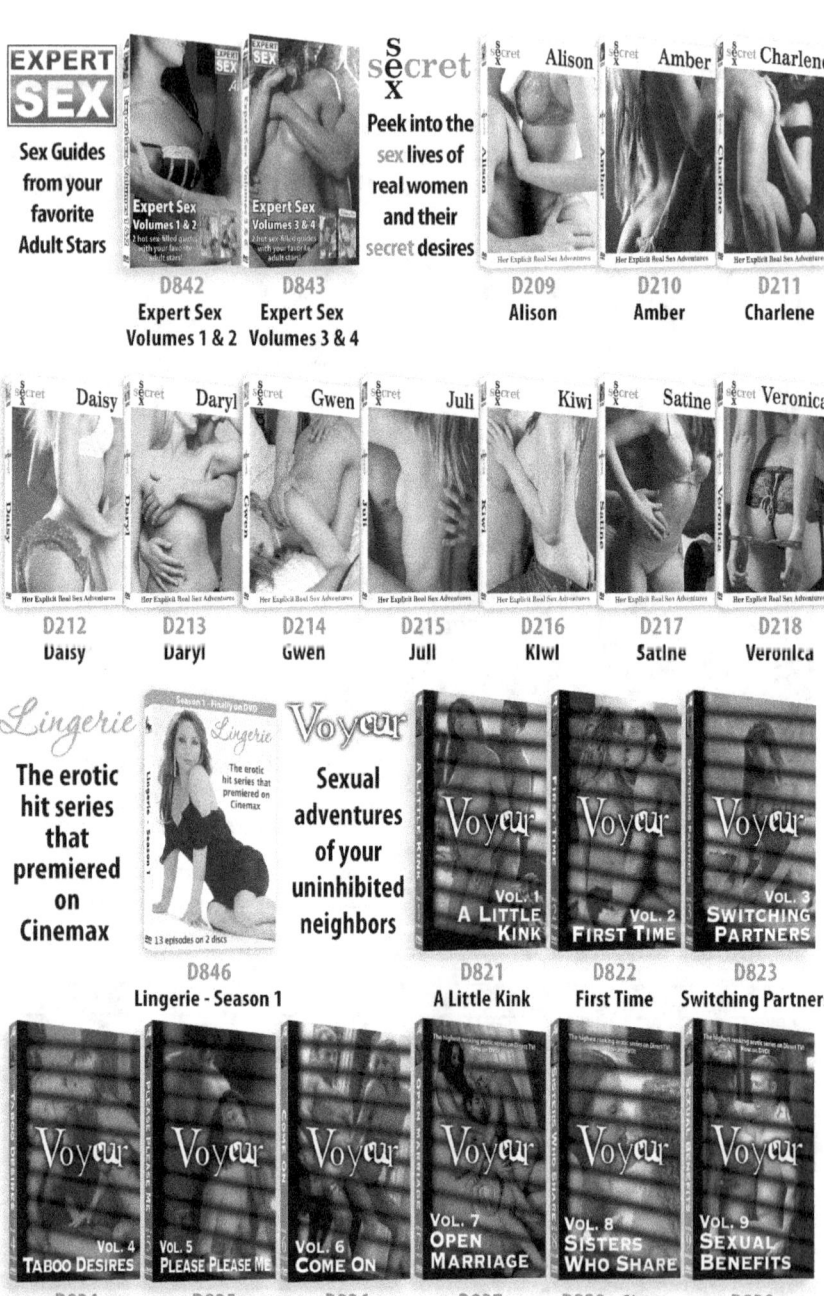

EXPERT SEX

Sex Guides from your favorite Adult Stars

Peek into the sex lives of real women and their secret desires

D842 — Expert Sex Volumes 1 & 2
D843 — Expert Sex Volumes 3 & 4

D209 — Alison
D210 — Amber
D211 — Charlene

D212 — Daisy
D213 — Daryl
D214 — Gwen
D215 — Juli
D216 — Kiwi
D217 — Satine
D218 — Veronica

Lingerie

The erotic hit series that premiered on Cinemax

D846 — Lingerie - Season 1

Voyeur

Sexual adventures of your uninhibited neighbors

D821 — A Little Kink
D822 — First Time
D823 — Switching Partners

D824 — Taboo Desires
D825 — Please Please Me
D826 — Come On
D827 — Open Marriage
D828 — Sisters Who Share
D829 — Sexual Benefits

UP TO 80% EXCLUSIVE DISCOUNT USING THIS FORM

DB401
Intimate Yoga for Couples Book
Over 270 Color Photos
with Sensual Yoga DVD

~~$45~~ $15

DB691
Erotic Stories Book with
3 Program/4 Hour DVD

~~$75~~ $12

DB650
Bondage Fantasies Book with
Endless Shades of Great Sex DVD

~~$35~~ $10

DT657
Endless Shades of Great Sex - 5 Item Kit
- Endless Shades of Great Sex Book
- Endless Shades of Great Sex DVD
- Masquerade Mask
- The Grey Tie
- Metal Handcuffs

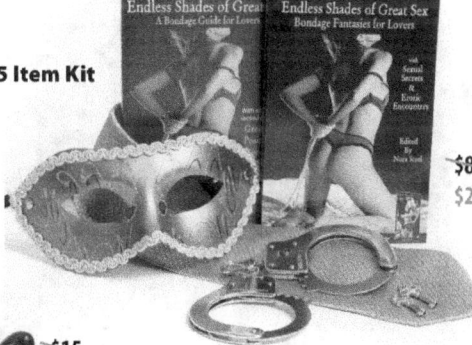

~~$80~~ $26

~~$20~~ $10

BT003
Prince Charming
Powerful, Quiet, Soft
Multi-Speed Vibrator

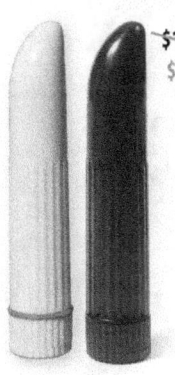

~~$15~~ $6

TPM02
Joli
Powerful, Multi-Speed
Classic Vibrator

~~$25~~ $9

BT006
Jewel Lipstick
Discreet, Powerful
Incognito Vibrator

~~$8~~ $4

BT301
1 oz Bliss Lube
100% Natural
Lubricant

~~$8~~ $4

BT302
1 oz Bliss Oil
100% Natural
Massage Oil

~~$24~~ $16

SE9709
Anastasia's Delight
Ergonomic, Silicone
Weighted Kegel Balls

SE9730
Athena
Discreet, Powerful
Multi-head Vibrator

~~$10~~ $8

~~$27~~ $16

SE9732
Romeo
Powerful, Vibrating
G-Spot Stimulator

~~$65~~ $45

T101
Powerful 10-inch
Variable-Speed
Wand Massager
with attachment

Millions Sold!

~~$15~~ $12

SE0782
Butterfly Kiss
#1 Selling
3-Speed Vibrator

Luxury Toys

~~$99~~ $79

T103
G-Vibe
Dual Stimulation
6-Function
Double Motor
Vibrator

~~$110~~ $79

T105
LEAF Vitality
Eco-friendly, Smooth
Dual Motor Vibrator

~~$76~~ $56

Millions Sold!

SE0610
Jack Rabbit Vibrator
5-Rows of Rotating Beads
Multiple Pulsations
and Rotations

~~$30~~ $24

SE2958
Showtime's Nick Hawk
Full Potential
Penis Pump

~~$190~~ $139

T106
Lelo Soraya
Attractive, Luxury
6-Mode Vibrator

~~$80~~ $64

T107
We-Vibe 2
Dual Stimulation
Couples Vibrator

~~$160~~ $119

T108
We-Vibe 4
6-Mode, Wireless Remote
The Ultimate Couples Vibrator

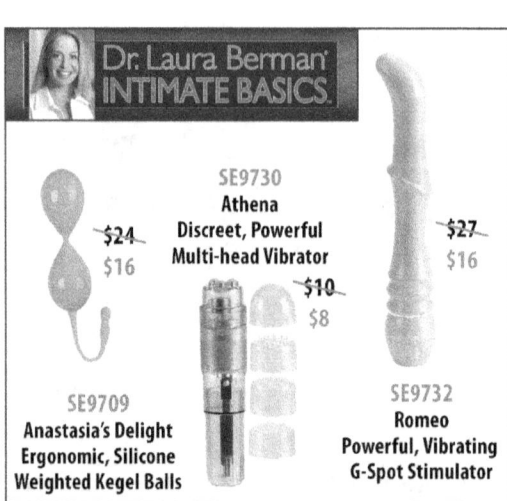

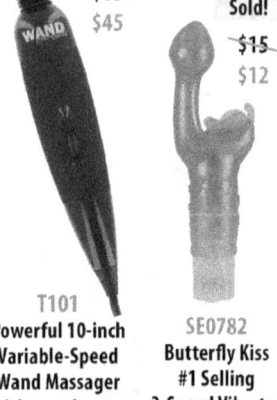

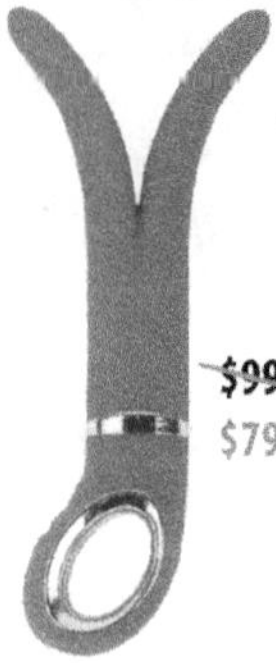

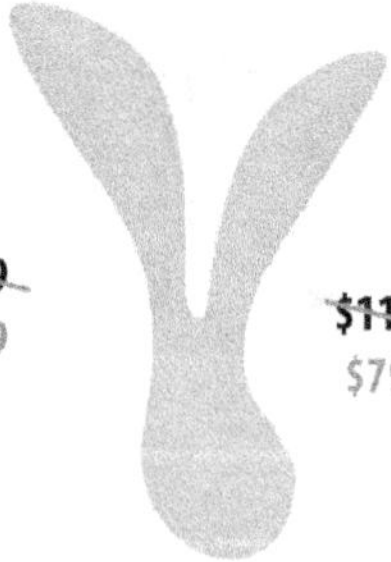

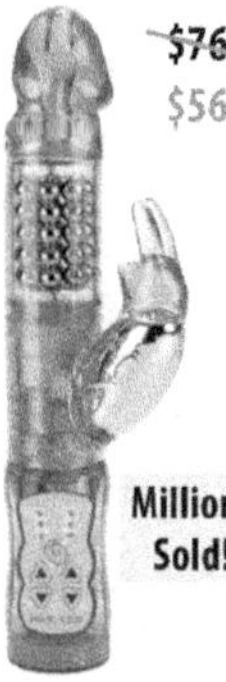

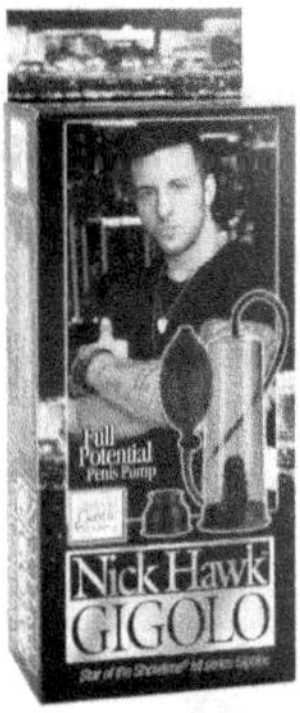

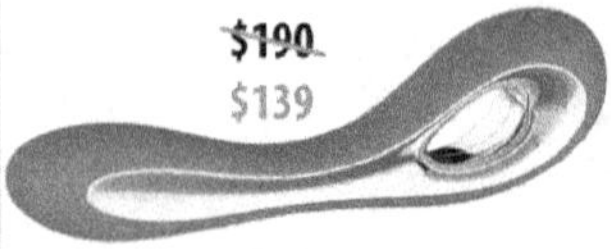

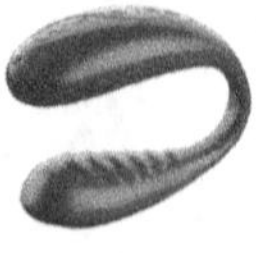

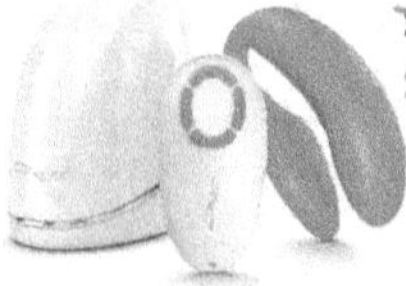